UBOA ACT 4

UBOA ACT 4

Prince Otchere

Contents

1

The Temptation

Adam was becoming more neglectful of his duties and responsibilities at home. He moved about with an air of careless and indifference his demeanor. Despite his proximity Adam seemed oddly distant from his family. He scarcely spent any time at home with his family was easily irritated and annoyed when provoked by with the slightest inquiry or suggestion. The sharp looks he received from his mate and son pierced and pained him dearly. The inner turmoil and feelings of resentment he harbored began to drive wedge between Adam and his family. Adam found himself drawing further away from the very people and place he regarded as his sanctuary and home. He preferred instead to spend much of his time in the pursuit of fulfillment of relaxation. His appetite for enjoyment and fun was often achieved during his daily travels and visits to the enchanting wonderland that was Eden. His mate and son were beginning to feel estranged. Adam behaved emotionally distant and void often alienating himself. He displayed little to no affection or concern towards his family. The family struggled to adjust to Adams condition of disassociation and lack of interest. They felt as though were being stonewalled and punished subjects of cruel and unusual treatment.

Adam ignored his family for the most part preferring to remain isolated and private whenever at home. He no longer held the same interest in his child and mate as he had in the past. Adam disregarded his family openly by being challenging and refusing to share common spaces or engage in civil dialogue with family members. Adam was growing rather neglectful and absentminded in his paternal role and duties. These oversights only helped to further intensify the already straining relationship. Adam no longer consoled or caressed his mate and often offered his backside to his partner whenever they slept. The soft and gentle caress of Adams touch went unfelt becoming less frequent. The affection and intimacy he had once showered and displayed for his partner was now absent in their relationship. The security and stability of companionship was steadily becoming a cause for concern with each passing day. Though Adam and his mate lived together and shared a dwelling the couple now seemed more estranged than ever. They behaved cavalier and unacquainted with each other rather than familiar lovers.

Adams presence in the home decreased significantly. He was now spending much of his time in pursuit of covert affairs. Adam set out daily in the pursuit and path of his desires and self-interest. He traveled beyond the great walls in search of adventure and fun while maintaining a friendly tryst. Adam was growing especially fond of the newly developed friendship he shared with Eve. He very much enjoyed basking in the ambiance of the creature's youthful glow and beauty. A long stroll through the large green estate became their daily routine. The two ventured about the land seeking out new and uncharted territories. One day Eve led Adam thru a secret path within garden. The quiet and quaint area nursed a collection of exotic flowers and plants. Eve explained that she had stumbled onto the floral paradise and secret garden during her exploration of Eden. Eve attended to the assortment of flowers which she curated and organized fancifully. She titled each specimen and strain in accordance with their characteristics. "I call these flowers there." Pointing to a nearby bush. "Amaryllis." She quickly shifted her fingers over to another bush. "And those deep pink ones are Anemone." Adam was fascinated not by the flowers in which Eve showed a great appreciation and understanding. He was more so moved by the eloquent and graceful way in which the nimble curator frolicked about.

The sound of Eve's voice was as pleasant to Adam's ears as was the sight of her beauty. In a sudden spark of excitement Eve snatched Adams arms pulling him through the flowery labyrinth into a quiet and isolated space deep in the heart of the maze. "Look at these." She turned to Adam showcasing another bushel of colorful flowers. "What are those?" Adam asked looking puzzled and confused unsure what to conclude. "Those are Alstroemeria flowers." Eve answered joyfully. "The rare plants cultivate in the oddest manner growing upside down." Adam could hear the excitement in Eve voice as she explained and specified the variations of flowers. Eve's face seemed to radiate and glow whenever Adam inquired or raised a question pertaining to the name, and origin of random flower bushels.

Adam entertained his friend teasing and making light-hearted jest of her pollinated infatuation. "Alright then." Adam declared proposing a fun and whimsical game. "What is that flower?" He asked pointing randomly at various strains of delicate flowers. Adam resembled an overbearing instructor examining the sharp wit and keenness of his most promising student and scholar. He intended to test the vastness of Eve's knowledge about botanicals and plant life. "What is this one?" Adam demanded quickly and shifting directions pointing at another bush "And that... And these... and those" Adam continued the exam trying desperately to stump and confuse the floral savant but failed miserably. Eve seemed unfazed by the bulk of random inquiries and questions posed by her jovial proctor. She spat out a name for every flower that Adams pointed out following in chronological order. "Lilly's, Pansies, Daises, Roses, Jasmines and Violets not to be confused for Lilacs despite their uncanny resemblance." Eve had answered intuitively leaving no reason or cause to deny her credibility.

Adam was impressed by Eves sharp wit and intellect. Her ability to recognize and name an entire flower garden was remarkably impressive. Adam admired Eve's mind and sharp wit. It was her proclivity to intellect that drew Adam affection. He often considered himself flawed and uncultivated whenever in Eve's presence. Adam reciprocated as best he could by sharing anecdotes and witty tales which drew gentle smiles and sweet laughter from the maiden. Adam exploited his reputation as an outlandish warrior and readily showed off his wounds and war scars to Eve. Each lesion and laceration contained its own triumphant story detailing his near-death encounter and experiences in the wilderness. He exaggerated the damage and injuries he sustained while hunting in the wildness. Adam honored his wounds by recognizing each scar as a badge of honor that demonstrated his many encounters and exploits at overcoming challenges and adversity. Adam was proud of the past struggles which he faced and persevered. The harsh conditions of the rough terrain had somehow helped to instill a sense of defiance and self-determination to not just survive but to also thrive in the wilderness.

Adam presented exemplary stories of his glorious conquests against the ferocious savages and monstrous beasts that dwelled outside of Eden. He demonstrated his battle skills by jabbing and swinging his arms around about madly with the chiseled object in hand. The sharply crafted tool that served Adam during his time of need was now being reduced to a mere prop that he used to animate and enhance his many stories. The wielding of the sharpened blade offered Adam a boost of energy and surge in vigor as he lunged the sharp dagger about. The unique demonstration helped to validate and verify the substance of his retellings. Eve found herself irresistibly fascinated by the gory illustrations of Adam's triumphant conquest. The gruesome description of his encounters appeared post traumatic as observed through Eve's eyes and lenses. Despite her observations Adam declared that the desolate environment awarded him a newly formed sense of awareness and heightened appreciation for life.

Adam accredited a large portion of his survival abilities to his neurotic sense of curiosity and resilience in the face of adversity. Eve's fascination with Adam drew interest to learn more about the species of wild savages that inhabited the world outside of the grand walls. Eve being like Adam was made and designed by God created within the confines of the mystical garden. Eden was the only home and world she had ever known. Eve retained the understanding that she was forever bound to the beautiful paradise for the rest of eternity. Despite never having seen or visited the outside world the creatures of Eden warned Eve on several occasions about the perils and dangers existing beyond the grand walls. However, the cautionary warnings did not stop her curiosity or detour her narrow imagination from dreaming up endless possibilities. Inside Eve's mind she imagined the world outside Eden preserved greener pastures and vast lands filled with wondrous creatures and beautiful scenery. Her inexperienced mind could not conceive or fathom the concept of barren emptiness. Innocently, Eve lacked the cynical depth and negativity to hold a destitute view of the world. She was unfamiliar with the notion and idea of suffering and hardship. The newcomer imagined the world being a picturesque and perfectly bonded like the botanical paradise she had come to know. However, after speaking with Adam these beliefs and delusions began to dwindle and subside after listening to Adam stories and experiences. Eve would eventually come to accept that there was no beauty or admiration to be sought after in the desolate lands.

Eve's interest and fascination with Adam seem to increase and grow with every meeting and interaction. She was enthralled by the wealth and depth of his knowledge and experiences. She was impressed by his tenacity and resilience of his defying will. Her admiration for Adam only rivaled that of Cain in the way she marveled over his adventures and conquest. Adam often recited action pack tales of his epic journey and encounters outside the grand walls. The colorful tales and stories he shared were filled with exaggerated heroism and embellished instances of heroic vigilance. Adam was masterful at weaving fanciful tales and wondrous stories from the depths of in his imagination. He composed stories which were met with scrutiny and criticism from Eve as well cross-examination. Adam found himself having to fabricate and falsify new tales to support the legitimacy of past and prior stories. Adam and Eve's relationship was a happy and blissful friendship that evolved innocently. The transition from platonic friendship into intimacy developed gradually into something much more. The two struggled to tame their growing interest and emotions feelings drawn by their swelling attraction. The natural flaw in their designs made them susceptible to both emotional and physical longing. The two would eventually surrender to feelings of desire, and unbridled lust swirling deep within them. These passionate interactions only helped to further Gods agenda. Adam and Eve's attraction offered the king somewhat of an advantage in furthering his plans. God provided the perfect conditions and environment for his precious creatures to flourish and grow. The magnitude of mutual interest made it nearly impossible for him to entertain the thought of escape. Adam plunged face first into the abysmal waters of redemption.

Tree took notice to the subtle changes in Adams attitude and demeanor. She observed the strange shift in his aura and energy. The prideful shame which Adam carried seem unbefitting of his character. In addition to her suspicions Tree began received updated reports from notable sources within the kingdom. The grass rooted community was filled with gossip and rumors pertaining to Adam and Eve love affair. The subject quickly drew popularity and began to surge as the most trending topic throughout the kingdom. Tree frequently received updates and reports from animals offering their eyewitnesses accounts. Very soon more locals turned up to share their testimonials to having witnessed Adam and Eve canoodling throughout the garden. Tree tried her best to ignore the salacious reports dismissing them as trifle misgivings and falsified allegations. However, the accusations placed against Adam and Eve were beginning to pile up against them. More creatures came forth to confess to having witnessed the two beings alone in the bushes engaging in extracurricular activities.

The bulk of unsolicited reports began to gain traction and soon developed into propaganda. They advertised and declared the union of Adam and Eve as blessed omen foreshadowing Adams triumphant return to the Eden. Tree was being bombarded daily with aerial reports from her feathery friends who confirmed flying over and viewing the romantic couple engaged in intimate dealings. Tree resented the loathsome remarks against Adams honor and would often deny the accusations and dismiss their speculations as unsubstantiated and highly improbable. She was growing rather annoyed with the cumbersome task of discerning the validity and authenticity of their heralded rumors. The constant alerts and notification defaming her dear friend began to irritate and disturb her inner sense of peace. Tree decided that she would confront Adam the next time the two were alone. She looked to gain clarity and hopefully dispel the loitering rumors as byproducts of misunderstanding and misinformation.

One day the opportunity to privately engage Adam presented itself as Tree finding herself alone with her dear friend. She decided it was the perfect moment to address the rampant rumors and hopefully disqualify the legitimacy of the false allegations. Tree steadied her nerves and racing thoughts. She chose her words carefully considering the possible backlash she could face for addressing the insidious scandal. "Adam," Tree called out to him, "I have noticed a sudden change in your behavior." Tree words brought with it a tense sensation of discomfort over Adam filling the space between the two friends with discomfort. Tree proceeded with caution very much aware as to the weight and gravity of the sensitive subject and topic. The least of her intent was to cause or bring offense to her dear friend. "What do you mean?" Adam answered back defiantly. Tree held her gaze fastened on his face sensing the growing temperament in his tone, "I am happy to see you so joyful, but I fear that you are forgetting your position." "My position." Adam repeated rhetorically,

"Yes, I fear you are beginning to neglect your family and your dutiful responsibilities. It appears you as escaping your obligations by spending most of your time here inside of Eden's walls."

Adam was outraged by the context of her declaration and at the time received the truth of her message as more of an insult. Tree's tone was stern if not firm and filled with genuine concern. Her rash delivery was not the subtle approach of minced wisdom diced to digest which Adam had grown accustomed receiving. If deemed possible a heavier layer of silence fell over the two that appeared to thicken the already tense air around them. Adam was speechless bewildered and frozen in dismay. He did not know what to say or how to react to her proclamation, "I am afraid." Tree continued. "That your newly acquired friendship is distracting you from attending to matters of equal importance. What has become of your domestic duties the role and oath you so readily upheld." Adam reflected of his family and quickly grew upset and annoyed imagining in his head the image of a son who mulled and mocked him with bitterness and contempt. He saw in his mind the face of his silent companion whose inability to speak or communicate emotions and feelings stiffened the potential growth of their relationship.

Tree for a moment seemed to forget the role and direction of her allegiance. She spoke to Adam as though he had unfastened the muzzle and filter that masked her true thoughts. Tree began speaking bluntly, "I am disappointed in you." Tree remarked. "The animals of the garden are gossiping and speaking recklessly about your conduct." Tree continued with her thoughts mildly unaware that her remarks were upsetting to Adam and making him Adam feel bad. "You have become the laughingstock of our community. You serve as a source of amusement for the creatures that inhabitant of Eden." Tree mocked playfully. However, before she could consider her actions Adam exploded, "How dare you Tree, stand before me thankless and ungrateful in your reproach." Adam was blatantly offended. "It would seem that you have already forgotten the fact that it was I who saved your life?" Tree was taken back by Adams outrage. "Have you forgotten how you bordered the brinks of death." Tears began to form slowly protruding beneath Adam's swelling eyes, "I set aside my pride and ego to plead before my estranged father begging that God restore you back to life." Adam was trying to shame Tree for her crude remarks.

"You say that I have abandoned my family," Adam stated loudly. "But that is because I spend the bulk of my time here looking over after you ensuring that you are well." Tree wanted to respond to Adam but did not want to further infuriate or irritate the fiery embers of his fiery temper. Adam had never held such a firm and boisterous tone against his dearest and beloved friend. The the heated moment of passion and conviction seemed to guide the temperament of Adams words and tongue. Adam's atrocious offenses seemed to penetrate Trees refined and hardened skin piercing deep into her heart. Her facial expressions began to melt over gradually forming into a piteous frown. Tree had never bore witness to the height of Adam's temperament or seen him in such an arrogant state. She wished she could simply expel the truth and confess her wrongdoings to help Adam. The disclosing revelation would offer Adam a possibly escape from the ploy unfurling against him." Despite her deep growing desire Tree could not find it her heart to unveil the diabolical plot against Adam.

Tree stood oddly frozen in silence filled with trepidation and fear of Gods wrath and retaliation if she dared to disclose or reveal his plans. The fact that Adam was being ensnared by seduction and manipulation was unsettling for Tree to endure. The truth and knowledge that Eve was purposely created as a pawn in Gods elaborate scheme to return Adam to the garden rested anxiously on her tongue barred by her lips. Tree struggled internally with the thought of expelling the truth. She resisted against the gnawing urge understanding very well that such an admission would be considered an act of treason that would ultimately warrant her demise and destruction. Adam took Tree's passive silence as permission to continue his hostile rant with amplified contempt. Adams flagrant tone and poor choice of words communicated the contempt beneath his messaging. The undertone tone of his message carried malice indignation within the embittering offense. Tree was heartbroken feeling torn apart by the very person she hailed as her own. The creature that she coveted and cared for most was now chopping her down emotionally limb by limb and root by root.

"Do you not want me here?" Adam imposed defiantly. However, Tree did not respond, nor would she speak appearing somewhat deafened by astonishment and grief. Tree was bewildered and surprisingly perplexed by Adam's rude and crass behavior. She repeated in her mind the harsh and unkind words which Adam spewed and spat at her. His sharp insults were painfully piercing but soon dulled into childish banter. Tree was slowly regaining her confidence and managed to evade the forceful gravity of Adam's emotional tantrum as an infantile attempted to distract her form concluding her speech. Tree was briefly derailed from her train of thought but was now back on track choosing to move forward with her point.

"I cannot answer that." Tree responded evasively. "That question is solely yours to answer." Tree did not intend to pursue a quarrel with Adam, nor did she wish to evoke hostility between the two. Tree did however want to address Adams unsound delusions. "If you wish to abandon your family." Tree remarked hastily. "That is your choice and decision to make and live with. But do not deceive yourself into believing that your daily visits to Eden were for my benefit or welfare." Tree actively recalled in her mind distinguishing the rarity of his visits when placed outside of Eden. "When you and I dwelled outside the gardens," Tree began to explain. "You rarely ever visited or sought my company. But now that I have been removed and stationed further away at the center of Eden. You find the will and time to visit more frequently in Eden. Why is that?" Tree was dueling skillfully within the arena of objectivity. She wielded reason and rational as her preferred weapon and tools of engagement. It was this trait and practice of mitigation that helped Tree to navigate and avoid unnecessary and senseless disputes.

Adams futile attempt to shift blame and deflect accountability was backfiring. He stood silent disarmed by the antiquity of Trees comprehension and wisdom. Intuitively Tree had anticipated one day encountering Adams cruel, and untamed persona. "I see now that I was wrong about you," Tree persisted. "You are afraid..." "Afraid!" Adam responded with laugher." "You of all creatures should know that I fear nothing. My dagger can attest to the query of my bravery." Tree was neither distracted or amused by Adams sorrowful attempt to once again derail her with needless and unnecessary interruptions. "You, Adam, are afraid of all that you have created. The ideals of family and connection which you once regarded openly no longer seem sacred to you. How can you not see that you have already won becoming the master of this world. You harness and possess everything that a being of your stature and caliber needs to survive and thrive despite the terrain or earthly conditions." Adam was moved by the depth of Tree's message and understood very clearly the moral subtlety of her loathsome address, "You have a loving partner and child who adore you" Tree reminded Adam. "Cain grows up more like you every day and very soon he will begin his search for his worth. I beg that you do not allow the cycle to continue. Do not allow Cain to grow up resenting his creator for his neglect and absence to then turn around to repeat the same mistakes."

Trees voice was her only weapon and tool she owned in her arsenal of defense. Her tongue was sharp, but her mind was much sharper. Her wisdom could easily sow the roots of fertile minds serving as the foundation and soil to help thoughts mature and grow. Her caring nature and warm temperament could easily be utilized to defuse contention and friction in the face of opposition. Trees words managed to cut through Adams emotional defenses piercing directly through his chest and heart. Adam felt embarrassed overcome by the sudden loss for words. He stammered, and stuttered pacing aimlessly about. He appeared unaccustomed to the daunting feelings of shame and remorse weighing over him. Adam darted his eyes and diverted his gaze. He resembled that of a sorrowful child trying desperately to hide his face. Looking down at the ground, Adam searched beneath his feet for a sensible rebuttal. He ravished through his mind for a legitimate argument to counter and bring forth but, found himself unable to produce a reasonable or sensible excuse for his behavior. The friction in the air was now tense between the two friends as moments passed with neither party speaking nor sharing a word.

It was only upon Eves sudden return did their attention avert from opposing directions refocusing their interest over to Eve. She walked towards Adam and Tree carrying in her arms a large bouquet of flowers she had hand-picked and gathered with the intention to surprising Adam with the thoughtful gift. As Eve walked closer, she could feel the heightened tension of awkwardness surrounding the silent pair. Eve instinctively sensed that something was wrong. "Is everything all, right?" She asked out loud, but no one offered to respond.

Finally, Adam broke the silence, "Eve, I must take my leave." He announced suddenly in a soft melancholy tone. "But why?" Eve asked. "The sun has yet to begun to set..." But before she could finish her thoughts Adam motioned his body slowly turning away to leave. Eve grabbed his arm unexpectedly stopping him. "Will you be return soon?" She asked innocently. Adam felt the unbearable weight of her Tree's gaze leering over him. He could not offer Eve a definite answer to her question and avoided looking directly into her direction. He slung his head downward away from the weary faces hiding his dampened eyes. Adam understood very well the prowess allure that Eve possessed over him beneath the enchanting effect of her gaze.

Adam's silent dismissal neither discouraged or detoured Eve from evoking a response. His questionable silence and strange behavior left Eve with the belief and perception that Adam would not be returning anytime soon. "I must go now," Adam declared pulling his arm away from Eve's grasp and turning his back to her. It was as though Adam was unwilling to bear the weight of distress drawn over Eve's saddened face. Adam understood very well that his relationship with Eve would only grow more intimate and complicated if he postponed his stay. "Wait..." Eve insisted. "At least take this." She attempted to hand Adam the bouquet of wildly decorated flowers, "I picked these out just for you." She lunged her arms outward to offer the beret of gorgeous flowers, but Adam would not respond or to turn around to accept the gift. Adam responded childishly reacting callous and cruel to the kind and heartwarming gesture.

The atmosphere surrounding the garden was sad and somber. Adam's decision to walk away from Eden was truly upsetting to watch and even more so difficult to endure. Despite giving Eve his back Adam could still hear from a distance the sound of her muffled outcry and weeps. Internally Adam wished desperately to sooth Eves sorrows but knew there was nothing he say could possibly say or do that could offer her comfort. He struggled against the temptation to look back at Eve one last time. However, he discouraged against the idea believing earnestly that the image of Eve in wallowing despair would only help to offset his agenda and delay his departure. The sight of Eve would ultimately make it more difficult for Adam to take his leave. Adam could hear Eve panting heavily but did not turn to acknowledge the suffocating agony of her present condition. He considered for a brief instance of accepting the floral arrangements. The large set of flowers beautifully twined and eloquently braided had been crafted and forged by Eve through the twilight and toilsome hours of the night. The decorative flower was largely fashioned as coronation rings resembled that of a besetting crown. The royal ornaments were largely designed as tailored head pieces befitting the ranks of nobility and royalty with Adam in mind.

Eve was upset by Adams behavior feeling the scorn of pain and humiliation in his unresponsive and distant demeanor. The sharp piercing feeling of unrequited love cut deeply leaving behind an emotional wound and scar over Eve's heart. The tense air surrounding them felt unbearably dense that Eve declared that she could scarcely breathe. She expressed symptoms of weakness appearing asphyxiated and somewhat short of breath. Eve would later account the terrifying experience as a panic attack of some sort. She later described the distressing event as a suffocating force attempting to smother her. Eves stretched-out arms collapsed slowly to her side as if daunted by the weight of the flowers in his arms. She appeared unable to wield the burden of ornamental flowers in her present state of sadness and despair. Eve loosened her grip to free the burdensome bouquet of floral decorations. In slow motion the rings of flowers dropped down on the ground landing gently against the heels of Adam's feet.

The sea of sorrow which Eve carried in her eyes had been finally breached resulting in an outpouring of tears. Like a faltering dam Eve felt the overwhelming force of rapid water running beneath her eyes. She found herself unable to control the current of rapid tears pouring down her dampened face. The shrieking pitch of Eve's outpouring ascended beyond the garden reaching the highest peaks of the mountainside. Her reaction exposed what the inhabitants of Eden had already surmised. Eve found herself confined within an emotional pit of disappointment and despair. It went without saying that Eve was hurt by Adam's blatant disregard for their bond and friendship. Adam, Eve and Tree shared the bulk of shame, pity and despair loitering over them. Further tension and discomfort ensued as Eve gazed upward to find a crowd of peering faces causally watching on with vested interest. There were clusters of creatures' mostly onlookers drawn forth by the sound of commotion. They strolled in and found seating beside their neighboring friends like an idling audience watching the climatic drama unfolding. The bane of Eve's turmoil and existence was now being channeled as a tragic comedy. Her pain and misery served as a source of entertainment for the inhabitants of Eden. Eve assumed the worse and was instantly consumed with embarrassment and humiliation over their mocking gaze. Eve looked on at the audience of spectators with loathing shame and self-pity. Eve blushed uncontrollably demonstrating that she was uneasy being placed beneath the spotlight of public scrutiny. The paddle of humiliation left Eve sorely defeated. Eve was left with no other recourse of action other than to flee and run away. She palmed her drenched face in attempt to mask her tears and remain hidden from the flagrant eyes of loitering faces. Eve removed herself from the present dilemma with a muffled outpouring before sprinting away.

Eve ran off stage escaping the swelling scene of contempt and disappointment which seemed to mock her very existence. Tree looked on at the ordeal and began to feel somewhat remorseful. She felt as though she should speak out and offer some form of resolve to mend the situation. Sadly, Tree could not muster any charitable or warm words that would pacify the downtrodden Eve. Evenly, she could neither produce nor dignify the genuine sentiments to console Adam. Eve furthered her distance while Adam lingered in the same spot somewhat frozen in grief. He appeared stationed by the imposition of derailing thoughts that seem to deflate his ego. Adam was reluctant to move his hesitation and cold feet seemed contrary to his boiling temper. Tree could not see Adams face visibly but knew with certainty that it was filled with tears.

Adam had not stirred or motioned his body for some time standing with his shoulders and body drooping down from the weight of his troubles. He finally stirred to motion his head down at the ground in view of the ornamental gift lying beside his feet. Adam quietly picked up the bouquet of flowers and without speaking another word he set forth on his path to return home. He stepped away with his chest and head held high walking tall and proud passing through the swarm of animals. The residents of the garden moved aside to create a path of egress for Adam to walk thru. Adam appeared unfazed by the cluster of wild animals and spectators engrossed in senseless chatter and gossip.

Externally Adam appeared calm and collected dignified only by his value and sense of self-worth. However internally he was distraught and heartbroken plagued emotionally by all that had occurred. As he walked on, he could sense all the animals mocking him with their gaze and soft whispers. The dull sounds of chatter and commotion faded away as he made his way through the large garden into the open fields. As Adam neared the passage leading out of Eden, he could not help but take notice of the strange change in the climate and weather. The sunny clear skies were now transforming into a morbid hue of gray that was beginning to cover the sky. The sound of loud rumbling filled the air observed by the formation and wave of robust clouds rolling across the sky. Suddenly without a warning a booming thunderclap exploded through the air that instantly startled Adam. The shattering sound was followed up by bursts of brightly lit bolts rippling across the sky. The intense demonstration of raging current was an unsettling to say the least. The fury of eruptions produced by the irritated clouds were profoundly alarming however not enough to discourage or deter Adam from leaving the garden. He could not recall ever having witnessed the skies transition and darken so rapidly during the peak hours of the day.

The clouds clumped together to form a thick layer of dark matter that eclipsed the sky casting a shadow over the land. Adam could scarcely make view of his path and landscape in front of him. He struggled to find his way carrying about aimlessly for some distance navigating through the darkness. A fiery bolt of lightning struck the ground just meters away from where Adam stood. The sudden spark startled Adam however, before he could react or collect his composure another thunder bolt flashed from high above striking down in the opposite direction. The bright spark of light though frighteningly fatal provided Adam the glimpse of light necessary to locate the exit leading out of Eden. He set forth in that path and direction towards the grand wall.

Adam appeared confused and very much spooked by the entire ordeal. He examined all that was taking place around him and quickly hastened his pace towards the exit. When Adam arrived home, he discovered his mate and child huddled together near the corner of the cavern den. They were seen comforting one another after having been impacted by the bellowing sound of roaring thunder that tormented the sky. The moment the family saw Adam enter the home they ran to embrace him in their arms. They rejoiced over Adam's safe return home by bombarding him hugs and kisses. Cain and his mother demonstrated their excitement by throwing the bulk of their weight onto Adam.

In one arm Adam firmly held his mate while tenderly embracing his son with the other. The heartfelt moment of joy and intimacy demonstrated his families love and adoration for him. Adam requited the display of love and affection by cradling both their bodies in his arms and showering them with soft pecks and kisses. He then presented his mate with a bouquet of exotic flowers, "I am sorry for my neglectful behavior as of late" Adam apologized, "I do not know what came over me." The simple apology caused droplets of tears to spill down his mate's face. The gracious smile of his endearing partner demonstrated compassion and forgiveness.

Adam turned his attention to Cain and gifted onto his son the floral ring that was intended for him. "I am sorry my son." Adam reconciled, "For I have failed you." This time the watery tears which were spewing down Adam's face. He fastened the flowery crown over Cain's temple adjusting it perfectly on his head. "I feel as though I have disappointed you, and I want to say..." But before Adam could finish speaking his son interrupted. "It is okay father..." Cain absolved Adam by wiping away the stream tears running down his face, "It is alright, we are together now father." Adam was moved and somewhat overcome with profound respect and admiration for his son. Cain was slowly maturing into sensible and wise young man, "Thank you son." Adam responded, looking into the eyes of his son before turning his attention back to his mate, "I cannot begin to explain the value of your forgiveness." Adam happily rejoiced grappling his family into his arms once again, "Thank you." He repeated the words like a mantra embracing his family tenderly while laying soft kisses.

They sat together around a warm bonfire listening to the thunderous soundtrack of anarchy echoing outside their home. The howling winds and gusty rainfall set a solemn and somber mood over the lands. They listened to the harmonizing sounds produced by the hailing storm scoring in the background. With the grumbling soundtrack of rolling thunder colliding over their heads Adam and his family nestled comfortably to together to rest. That night Adam reflected privately within the chambers of his private thoughts. He had overcome the challenges and difficulties that he endured by sheer will and determination. The very will he used to overcome adversity as a skillful huntsman prevailed to restore his sense of purpose and identity. Adam rejoiced with glee at the thought of rediscovering the joys of domestication. All seemed to be going well for Adam after reclaiming the self-appointed role as provider and protector of his family and home. Like a blooming flower Adam flourished bountifully surrounding himself with producers of the rare mineral love.

In overcoming the challenging ordeal and experience Adam felt reunited and somewhat more connected with his family. The emotional baggage and distance which kept Adam away from his family was slowly being unpacked. The emotional alchemy of transform his feelings of guilt and shame into tenderness and closeness was no easy feat. Adam became an advocate for quality time encouraging the practice and routine of family bonding. He appeared aggressive in his recovery and was eager to return to his usual happy and grateful self again. Occasionally he experienced haunting dreams brought on by unresolved feelings of remorse and guilt. The dreary images which appeared in his dreams served as guilty reminders of the life and world in which he left behind. Some nights Adams thoughts roamed freely only to return to the garden where he replayed the contentious incident over in his mind. He appeared unsettled the divisive interaction Tree and Eve and himself. Adam struggled to accept the notion that he had in some way wrongfully dishonored them.

2

The Awakening

As time went on, Adam found his thoughts drifting away frequently wandering off into the realms of Eden. He often thought about his encounter with Tree recalling the exchange of harsh words last shared between them. Adam contemplated considerably thinking of the various ways in which he could have resolved the entire ordeal. These sincere thoughts led him to ponder over Eve recalling the indecency of his behavior and offense. A host of unsolicited memories began surface in Adam's mind which troubled and disturbed the solace and peace he sought desperately to preserve. He attempted to suppress the resurfacing images of Tree, Eve and the entire community of Eden from invading his thoughts. Adam wanted nothing more than to live happily with his mate and son. He was satisfied if not content accepting the mundane routine of domestic life. He had for the most part successful and doing did well in his deliberate efforts to ignore and remove Tree and Eve from his thoughts.

Adam managed well in the daytime seeing as he was awake and able to control his conscious thoughts. The nighttime was when Adam faced the most difficulty as he struggled internally to fall and stay asleep. He rarely obtained a full night's rest before being transported to a lucid dreamworld. The restful state of sleep relinquished his control over his subconscious thoughts as his mind roamed freely without limits or boundaries. In his vivid dreams of Eden Adam pictured the rarest and most exotic flowers surrounding bountiful pastures of greenery. These images he conjured in his dreams often placed him somewhere within the permeable landscape of Eden. Adam found himself powerless to defend against this insidious inception of his mind. The disarming act of falling asleep resigned his sense of reason and judgment.

Adam was plagued in his dreams to the point that he seldom took time to rest. On many nights he tossed and turned in his sleep trying desperately to escape the nightmares which cursed and haunted his dreams. Adam's body soaked profusely with beads of warm sweat covering his moist body like morning dew. He often awoke to discover his body drenched lying atop a damp bed. When approached by his family who came forth to express their worries and concerns Adam would often minimize and deflect to offer passive reassurance to his family that he was fine and well. He provided a plausible explanation declaring that the excess of moisture and sweat was primarily due to the dense humidity of the nights air.

The reoccurring dreams began to take an effect over Adam as he was often taxed and depleted of energy. Adam's deprivation and noticeable struggle with sleep was beginning to take a toll over his mental and physical health. His weary demeanor and fatigued disposition made him appear observably slow and lethargic in his demeanor moving around sluggishly. Most days Adam would be at home pacing back and forth through the cavern. When plagued with fatigue or exhaustion Adam took refuge in his usual seating area where he proceeded to sit for hours. Adam could be found many nights sitting in perfect stillness with his chin resting over his fist immersed in deep thought. The seated position lacked the necessary comforts for a restful kip but nevertheless the practice of stillness provided him solace and inner peace.

Adam was opposed the thought of completing a full night's sleep and often fought against his body's natural urge and call to rest. Adams sought desperately to remain awake throughout the moonlit hours very often at the expense of his well being. He was depriving himself of the vital necessity and benefits of rest. Despite his willful efforts Adam struggled to stay awake often confronted by the daunting weight of exhaustion. Adam begrudgingly contested the dwindling feeling of tiredness that evoked in whenever confronted by exhaustion. He struggled desperately to shake away the feeling of fatigue and weariness dawning over him. It was not long before Adam would succumb to the burly weight of deprivation. His weary brows and tired bones growing heavy and dense with fatigue served as an indication that Adam that had reached his nocturnal peak and was rapidly approaching the brink exhaustion. He would soon find himself drifting off passing in and out of consciousness teetering back and forth between the earthly realms and that of his dream world. Adam toggled his head in denial as if fighting against his fatigue and need to sleep. He swayed his head back and forth in disagreement until finally a hard jolt and swift turn of his head collapsed his body sending Adam tumbling into a much-needed state of slumber and sleep.

One morning during the late midnight hours Adam's companion awoke to find him hunched over against the entrance way. Adam looked exhausted and was observed nodding off falling in and out of consciousness. He fought back against the temptation to sleep refusing to succumb to call of sleep. His mate took notice to Adams struggle observing the beads of sweat that formed over his body. The worrisome creature drew alarm and panic viewing Adam's excessive profusion as a symptomatic indication of an unknown ailment. His mate moved quickly to secure a dry cloth to wipe away the glossy glare of moisture off his body. The gesture provoked a startling reaction and sudden outcry and loud scream from Adam's lips "Please forgive me!" He cried out shaking frantically and curling himself into a ball. He cowered backwards shielding his face and body as though protecting himself from an onslaught of invisible strikes and blows.

Adam quaked feverishly on the ground overcome by delusional fears that seemed to erode his senses. Crippling fear caused Adam to resist the helpful hands of supportive partner. Like any individual engulfed within a traumatic nightmare Adam refused to open his eyes. A moment of relief finally came as he felt the gentle touch of his mate caressing his back. His eyes which were tightly clamped and closed shut began to slowly pry open. "Oh my." Adam quickly recovered. "It is only you." He exhaled a heavy sigh of relief. Adam's declaration prompted a strange gaze from his mate which seemed to express and capture in essence the very words in which the creature could not speak.

"Who else would it be?" Adam quickly deflected before accepting his mate's helpful hand and support with getting onto his feet. Adam's mate attempted to lead him back to bed however resisted against the idea. "I would prefer not to sleep." Adam explained. "As a matter of fact, I am no longer weary you see." He raised his brows to expose the sleep deprived and blood shot eyes both of which he could scarcely keep open. The drooping set of baggage's he carried beneath his brows demonstrated the depth of his exhaustion.

Adam chattered on but found himself yawning after a few short words. His slow and drowsy demeanor revealed the truth he sought desperately to conceal. That he had not had full nights rest for nearly a fortnight. One could easily observe that Adam was distressed just by gazing at him. He was unable to produce a plausible excuse to explain his sudden affliction of restlessness insomnia. Adam alluded further away from the unspoken question of his deprivation into subjects and topics that served no value or importance. His mate attempted with the best intentions to stay up with Adam however the heaviness of the night was beginning take an effect over the poor creature. Adams yawns were becoming quite contagious but unlike Adam his mate was prepared to act on the feeling and return to bed. The weary creature accepted that whatever ailed Adam he would speak on it when he was ready.

Just as his mate was preparing to take leave and return to bed Adam reached out suddenly. "Wait, since you are already awake." Adam suggested. "Why not stay up with me." His mate stared questionably at Adam as though confused by his strange request. Adam was met with beaten brows and skepticism. The odd request was met with scrutiny over his strange and peculiar behavior. It was the unbearable weight of his partners silent gaze that Adam found unbearable to endure. "Words are easy." Adam declared. "They can be changed, corrected and obscured to have several interpretations. However, silence when used appropriately possesses the ability to dismantle the toughest armor and penetrate the strongest defenses."

Adam sat with his mate beneath the glowing moon watching the starlit sky. The indescribable feelings of peace and serenity began to dawn over him. The warm and soothing feelings served well to shield him against the brisk blight of the brisk night air. Ultimately it was the perplexing look of concern and confusion that he received from his concerned partner that moved him to speak out and disclose and reveal the truth. At first Adam's jabbering was taken as another forlorn attempt at keeping them awake and occupied. But as Adam spoke it was apparent that he was lucid in his thoughts somehow provoked by the will to share the source of his turmoil and troubles. Adam expected very little to come from his interpretive telling as he attempted desperately to retain the interest and company of mate. He reserved the belief that his partner could somehow serve as supportive figure and a listening ear. The fact that the two could never share meaningful discourse or dialogue did not detour Adam from enjoying the comforting presence of his mate. Adam partner's company was useful in keeping him distracted from the howling winds calling for his resignation.

"I have strange dreams." Adam disclosed openly. "No, rather they are nightmares." He clarified. Adam searched his partners face for indications and signs of exhaustion and fatigue. Surprisingly Adam discovered his mate wide awake and patiently waiting for him to unpack the bulk of his troubles. The sentimental moment was captured between lovers. Adam received a nod of encouragement from his partner which served as his signal and cue to continue.

"In my dreams I see Tree," Adam revealed. "Standing off in the distance placed near a barren cliff. She looks bruised and battered, however, I am too far away to see her face clearly, and so I walk to her. And as I am moving closer a foul smell fills the air around me. The putrid stench reeked profusely forcing me to cover my face and shield my nose from the nauseating stench. Despite the distance between us I could hear Tree crying out to me in pain, "Adam!" She pleaded repeatedly. "Help me, please!" The pungent scent resembled that of a potent greasy odor that filled the air. I try to run to her side." Adam continued. "But my legs stiffen and cramp up quickly so that I am unable to move despite all my effort. I feel drawn to the sound and direction of her echoing outcry ringing loudly through the air. My feet struggled to navigate the thick murky ground treading carefully through the dark muddy terrain. The exerting task of walking through the mud felt daunting and perilous. I struggled to maneuver through the slimy thick mosh that engulf my ankles and feet. When I stopped to look down at my muddied heels, I was shockingly disturbed to discover that my toes and feet completely stained with clots of blood. I followed the trailing path of blood leading uphill only to uncover the running trail running up down the cliff where Tree was stationed."

"I furthered my pursuit with relentless determination. I was committed to pushing myself forward and overcoming the challenges and obstacles set before me. I managed to reach the shore and started up the steep hill towards Tree. I manage to edge closer to the top of the steep hill where I am confronted and faced with true extent of Trees pain and suffering observed by her withering and decaying body. Tree looked as if she had been improperly pruned and brutally assaulted like a victim of some heinous and violent crime. She was severely battered and badly bruised with large ink blots covering most of her body. Her wounding marks showed welts and ridges carved beneath her bark skin. The temperature suddenly changed as the tepid winds began to blow cool air over the land. I can still hear Tree's teeth chattering loudly through the air. Her trembling body shivering feverishly from the sudden rush of brisk air. Her decrepit posture and burly branches hunched downward cracking and snapping apart from the impact of forceful winds that blew. I fought against the heralding winds drawing close enough to view firsthand the look of pain and distress on my dearest friend face. Tree was crippled with agony her merciful tears poured down the side of her face. The unnatural pitch of her outcry brought a shiver through my spine and body. Her agonizing cries and wrenching calls for forgiveness could be heard echoing loudly through the air. I nursed feeling of helplessness and inadequacy over my failure to offer support or assistance to Tree during this dire time. My diligent efforts seemed futile by this point, however I refused to give in. I persisted forward in pursuit of fulfilling the lofty goal of being by her side.

I managed to reach close enough to call out to Tree just before a strange phenomenon suddenly begins to take place. Astonishingly the earth beneath my feet begins to rumble and shake violently with increased momentum. The fierce quake caused the ground to crumble and collapse before my very eyes. The ground began to severe and break apart forming a gaping hole. The unabridged gorge only helped to further the distance and divide between Tree and myself. I considered the amazing feat of hurdling myself over the gaping hole to reach the other side. However, as I prepared to stake my mark without provocation or cause lava and fire begin to erupt violently into the air. As if the present circumstances of my perilous dilemma were not already dire the appearance of molten lava began to spill over and ooze out from the trenches of the gaping hole onto the land. These were the conditions in which I faced and struggled to overcome. The worse part of it all was that I could still hear Tree crying out to me.

I could feel the sweltering heat and humidity heat and hot air bask over me. The thicket of steaming fog temporarily clouded my vision however did little do stifle Tree calls to me. Her outcries echoed louder with every agonizing call. I searched the hot dense fog and managed to locate Tree. She was lying helplessly lamed on the cliff beyond the limits of my reach and support. Tree was confined to the ruins of a lonely cliff side separated by fire and earth. I felt haunted being forced to endure the pleading woes and sorrowful outcries of my loyal stewardess and guardian. Confronted with the rapture of Tree piteous cries I became suddenly conflicted and consumed with unbridled anguish. It pained my very heart to hear Tree crying out for me. I dug my finger into my ears in attempt to end the wailing cries, but somehow this did not work. "Adam!" Tree cried out in a famished and feeble voice. She managed to breach the barriers of my clogged defenses with her pouring outcry. The hurt and pain in her voice was filled with torment and agony. I wept and plead that she would find a grain of relief from all her suffering. "Help me, Adam!" Tree cried out again. She begged for me to somehow come to her rescue, but I was helplessly pitiful and cowardly in my apprehension to act. My hesitation was justified in my fear of sustaining severe injuries burns and wounds. I did not shy away from considering the morbid extreme that my efforts would conclude with grave outcomes. The mournful realization of my fearful cowardliness caused tears to flush down my face.

The intolerable pitch of Tree's pouring outcries had finally reached its pinnacle. The torment of shame which I carried beneath my chest and bosom soon formed into bitterness and anguish over my submission and defeat. Surprisingly those very emotions that provoked guilt of shame would help free me from the shackles of fear and trepidation which convicted me. The very acceptance of my demise in exchange for the life of my dearest friend no longer sent chills to through my body. No rather it had the opposite effect serving as a source of inspiration. I made up my mind right then and there that I would risk my life to save Tree. I heaved a heavy gust air as I prepared myself for the jump. I started off by distancing myself several feet from the fiery pit. I moved backwards until I secured the necessary traction and space to propel my footing to execute the extraordinary leap.

I sped towards Tree's direction running with as much speed and agility as I could muster. Rapidly approaching the fiery pit, I lunged into the air. I soared over the scorching edge and for a moment I felt weightless moving over the bubbling pit of fire. Flying thru the air with my eyes fixed and fastened on Tree I soared with grace and ease. However, while in the air something in the distance derailed my attention. Looking off yonder I thought I recognized a familiar face. The very instance I withdrew my gaze from Tree I began to fall and plummet downward into the mouth of the burning cliff. It is at this point that I awaken to find myself bathing in moist dew moistness and sweat. Would you believe that I have attempted the impossible leap several times in my dreams and each time I have managed to fail miserably. The descent of my sorrows and troubles weighs over on me like heavy stones pulling me down into the fiery pit. Still to this day I have yet to reach Tree on the other side of that cliff. The vivid image of Tree left alone and abandoned on top of that cliff haunts my thoughts. I see her face whenever I close my eyes and attempt to sleep. Unfortunately, I have no control over my dreams and continue to endure and experience the same wretched inception."

"The worst part of it all," Adam confessed openly. "As of late I am no longer able to determine whether my bountiful leaps are genuine attempts to rescue Tree, or simply masked ideations to end my life and awaken from the insufferable nightmare." Adams voice flustered as he spoke. "It just doesn't make sense." He cried, "I curse my crafty mind which taunts me so. On many occasions the gaping pit appeared manageable sometimes stretching no longer than a simple foot apart. And if I attempted to leap across the small gap instantly expanded opening wide like a mouth ready to swallow me entirely. Even though I can never seem reach the other end of the cliff. I often wondered to myself had I managed to execute the impossible feat of making it across to her. How would I have been of any use or service to Tree. What could I do to help or aide her from her troubles. I accepted the trivial reservations of my self- doubt and pity with neglect and indifference.

These emotional weights only helped to sink me further into the fiery abyss. The bulk of my burdens and fears served to be obstacles and barriers which inhibited my plight..."

Dawn was rapidly approaching, and Adam was near exhaustion and scarcely unaware of the already collapsed body of his mate resting peacefully against his side. "All I have to do is keep my eyes on Tree..." Adam declared giving out a huge and exhausting yawn, "But I seem to always fail." Highlights of historical failed attempts replayed over in Adams weary mind until finally he gave up and gave out another ghastly yawn before collapsing alongside his mate.

On this cathartic night Adam slept peaceful and sound. His thoughts and dreams were tranquil and serene. The endless cycle of nightmares that plagued him nightly did not appear in his sleep. Adam did not awaken as usual in a pool of sweat and damped bedding. It was difficult to determine whether Adams candid confessional served as a therapeutic sedative resembling the most primitive form of counseling. The sharing of emotional turmoil and strife seemed to offer Adam relief from the overwhelming distress and feelings of guilt, fear and shame. All these emotions Adam harbored deep within his tormented soul. But for now, it seemed that Adam was able to sleep comfortably once again or so he believed.

3

The Revelation

The next morning Adam returned to Eden with the intention of apologizing for his crude and crass behavior. He could no longer sit with the intense feelings of shame and guilt which he unintentionally harbored. Adam was unwilling to entertain the begrudging emotions stirring deep inside of him. However, upon entering Eden and arriving and at the garden Adam did not find Tree in the usual place or station. The plotted area where she once occupied and stood was now an empty and desolate space. Adam looked around confused as to the strange disappearance of his friend.

Eve appeared suddenly strolling idly through the garden. She appeared bewildered with astonishment and surprised to find Adam standing exactly where she had last seen him. "Adam!" She called out taken aback by his unannounced arrival. Adam looked up and saw that it was Eve calling out to him. She arrived at his side nearly out of breath and her face filled with tears. "I am so sorry." Eve apologized mournfully. "I just... I mean... I did not know..." Adam was quite confused by Eve's ramblings but as he continued to listen it became clearer what had taken place and occurred during his absence.

"Tree was only following orders." Eve behaved hysterically somewhat erratic in her delivery. " Wait, what." Adam questioned. "Who's orders? I do not understand." "His lordship. I mean your father." Eve responded. "My father" Adam repeated in utter shock. "What does God want with me." "Your father." Eve began. "Has hatched a dastardly plot against you," Adam looked riddled with confusion. "It was God who requested the locket of your mate's hair not Tree." "But, why?" Adam questioned still struggling to fully comprehend the gravity of Eve's message. "Tree disclosed before her disappearance that God conjured a plan to remove you from your family. She shared that a locket of hair you bestowed onto you by as a gift. And that our master was successful in his efforts to replicate and create another companion for you." "Adam!" Eve called out to him suddenly with heightened hesitation. "It appears that I am the very creature and companion crafted and designed specifically for you."

Adam was astonished somewhat floored by the startling revelation and discovery. The turmoil of betrayal and heartbreak cast a looming shadow over him. Adam grew nauseous and slightly winded panting desperately for air. "Why does my father taunt me so!" Adam lashed out. He dropped to his knees over the plot of land where his best friend once stood. "Why does he taunt us so?" Adam asked looking over at Eve. "Why not create another creature in my place," Adam sobbed. Eve could sense that Adam was very much distressed by the unveiling of Gods plot and scheme against him. She and attempted to offer Adam comfort and resolve by answering question to his inquiries.

Eve began to explain "I was told by Tree that God has the ability can create and form any creature he desires. However, as it was explained and understood by me that your mate is a unique creature of which God did not mold or create in his design. The rationale that if your mate was not crafted by our master and king then the creature must have been fashioned by the hands of his nemesis." Adam gave a cautionary gaze that resembled a cold stare as if warning Eve to tread carefully in her approach. The scornful glare encouraged Eve and to be more selective in her sparing delivery. Eve acknowledged the frigid look with an unspoken understanding that she had faltered in her delivery and poor explanation. She attempted to recover from the shade of jabs by offering a halfhearted apology which Adam appeared reluctant and indifferent to accept. "God had no idea." Eve continued. "That his nemesis would try to destroy the bulk of his work and endeavors by creating a…" Eve sought it best to reevaluate her thoughts and correct her words, "I am sorry Adam, but your mate is nothing more than an archetype replica of you." Silence fell between them. "Can't you see that the creature embodies your design with only a few minimal differences in structure and composition."

"Enough!" Adam raged, "I have heard enough, do not feed me any more lies!" He was prepared to bring an end to the conversation by abruptly making his exit. But before he could step away Eve grabbed onto his arm. "Please listen to me for I fear this may be last time that we speak. I have said too much." At hearing Eve's admission Adams body reacted instantly and froze in response. The thought of God removing Eve chilled Adam to his core. He found it nearly impossible to step away or remove himself from Eve.

"I thought that you should know the truth." Eve began again, "So that you may have peace, and closure in your mind and heart. I am only offering knowledge as it was shared with me by our noble friend Tree. Trust and believe that she confided in me all that I have shared with you. My aim and intentions are to offer you solace and resolve for your grief and loss, as well as to bring honor to the life and legacy of Tree." Eve's aura and presence had been sorely missed. Her kind and gentle words helped to sooth him though the overwhelming process of grief and loss. Adam was gravely troubled by the removal and loss of his dearest friend. He felt helpless and hopeless uncertain as to what he should believe. Adam's intuition and conviction retained the belief that something was off, and that Eve was not presenting him with the truth in its entirety. He sensed that she was withholding and keeping something back from him.

Adam sighed with disappointment drawing air into nostrils his lungs before exhaling his frustrations. He seemed exhausted and somewhat numbed by the distressing news. He drew in another heap of air and exhaled slowly letting out the air of tension and frustration which seem to be building deep beneath his chest. "Continue," Adam requested impatiently. "Share with me all truths that Tree has unveiled to you." Eve took Adam's growing interest and request as a verbal cue and consent for her to continue. "It is extremely difficulty and nearly impossible for God to design a creature as…" Eve paused to choose her words carefully as not offend Adam. "…perfect as your companion. And had our mighty king originally conceived and formed your mate than your partner would be sanctioned." "But how can this be when God is the creator and archetype of all things." Adam rebutted. "That he is." Eve agreed. "However, as Tree explained it the universe is governed by a set of principles described as spiritual laws. The laws serve as the foundational guidelines and basic instructions for crafting and creating new life." Adam looked on at Eve confused and somewhat baffled mostly perplexed by depth of his own ignorance at the notion of spiritual law. "What is this spiritual law?" Adam requested to know as to avoid seeming further ignorant on the subject matter. "Spiritual law," Eve answered. "As I understand it, is a governing decree which forbids omnipotent creators and forces the supernatural authority to infringe on another's design and creation. Spiritual law ultimately forbids the duplication and replication the same creature more than once. The sacred proscribed policy assures that only the founder and true architect can assume spiritual property. Only the founder has the liberty and right to adjust and make modifications to an original design."

This explanation did not help Adam as he looked more puzzled over the topic than when he had initially inquired. "You see." Eve added. "The law upholds when reversed. God's nemesis is incapable of forging another creature of your exact image and design because of spiritual law. Man being God's celestial property grants him domain and proprietorship over you." Adam listened to the long-drawn-out rhetoric and soon his head began to pang and throb. He attempted to sort thru and comprehend the bulk of information and intelligence he was receiving.

Adam pondered silently on what to make of Eve's report. "My partner is dear to me." Adam explained irritably, "It is foolish to think that I would ever abandon or forsake my mate." A rather perplexing and disturbing thought suddenly surfaced Adam's mind instantly filling him with discomfort. "And what of my son" Adam expelled stoically. "What ridiculous laws binds Cains loyalty?" He searched Eve's eyes and face desperate for a sensible repones but found her seemingly uncertain. "Spiritual law." Eve attempted to explain. "Would consider Cain to be a combinational hybrid of his creators. However, it is difficult to foresee or predict exactly which inherent traits or attributes he has inherited. I am afraid I cannot say for sure." Eve paused for a moment looking directly into Adam's face but could not meet his eyes. "I am sorry Adam." Eve apologized lowering her head in shame as if burdened by the limits of her knowledge.

Adam did not speak but stood poised gazing off into nothingness. He appeared distracted and somewhat disassociated from the present moment staring directly into the abysmal darkness. Adams thought began to roam freely soaring high above him. His mind shifted over the barren trenches and wasteland to the cavern dwelling he regarded and called his home. Adam thought of his mate and son and having nearly lost them to God's delinquent scheme. The climactic moment of silence finally ended with Adam breaking the awkward tension. "Eden is no longer my home." Adam professed openly. "My heart no longer yearns for the garden." Adam paused as if inspired by the breadth of his sudden revelation. "My loyalty belongs wherever I can live free and love as I choose and see fit. My mate and son are all that I have in the wretched world, and against odds they are all I need by it. I will not attempt to explain the love and joy that my family brings me despite my many shortcomings. I have come to accept that there are no peaceful settings or harsh conditions in this world. The alchemy and magic of a loving family can transform the desolate scenery of the outskirts into a wondrous setting and paradise."

As Eve listened to Adam's words, she began to realize that the love and regard that Adam reserved for his family was truly immeasurable. They held a bond that neither Eve nor God could tear apart. "I understand it now." Eve responded empathetically. "And I am inclined to agree with you. It is not right what God is doing to you. I was pawned and used as a tool of seduction by our king, so that you may be subject to his mercy and will." Adam felt awkward for he knew very well that Eve would be subject to a severe and harsh punishment for her flagrant act of treason. "What wiil come of you?" Adam turned to Eve appearing concerned. "What will you do when God discovers that you have failed your mission and were unable to persuade me to stay?" Eve was nervous and trembling desperately with fear, "I do not know." She responded hysterically. "How will you answer when your king questions you over the context of our discourse? " "I do not know." Eve cried out overcome with emotion. By now Adam was beginning to lose his temper and was growing rather annoyed and upset, "What do you mean you do not now," Adam shouted angrily "Have you seriously not given consideration to the backlash and repercussions that will ensue from this act of betrayal?" The harsh tone of Adams scolding was enough to bruise and batter Eve's fragile and delicate ego. She suddenly burst into whimpering tears. Adam was growing more irritated and annoyed by Eve's emotional reaction. He was stifled by the sight and image of Eve wailing and grieving pitifully. She attempted to outsource compassion and sympathy from the barren mines of Adam's desolate and empty heart.

Adam saw no use in hurling his frustrations at Eve when in truth he knew very well that he could not protect Eve from Gods wrath. He also knew that he could not offer her refuge by bringing her home to live with him and his family. Adam's keen insight could already foresee the snaring pitfalls that would ensue from such a rash decision. The addition of Eve in his home would only help to further complicate the dynamics of his family and home. Adam could already imagine and foresee the tumultuous outcome. He was almost certain of the fact that his feelings for Eve would overshadow his affection for his mate. Adam submitted to thought and chose to avoid the foretelling act of betrayal. "I am unsure what I will say or do when God's confronts me." Eve answered pitifully in a meek and docile voice. "You see Adam..." Eve paused with some hesitation, "I am with child."

Eve's announcement rung loud like a bell echoing between Adams ears. He became lightheaded and nearly collapsed on the ground from the bewildering and surprising news. Adam assumed that he was being deceived and took Eve's report as a deliberate hoax. He viewed the reveal as a poorly orchestrated and immoral attempt to keep him confined in Eden. Adam felt as though he had been manipulated and used like a simple cog in an elaborate sham. He began to question the odd number of players and actors who conspired and colluded to unfurl this fiendish plot. It was too early to tell whether Eve's announcement would become Adams undoing at the time. The earthshaking news stunned and rattled Adam to his core understanding very well the severity and gravity of his present circumstance.

If deemed as truth the shocking news would ultimately postpone Adam's resignation and withdrawal from Eden. He was upset and seemingly outraged for allowing himself to be baited and snagged into such a sinister scheme and ploy. Adam took personal offense to his betrayal and for a moment wrestled with his inner conscious He demonstrated his struggle by examining his role and position in the play of lies and deception. Adam began to reevaluate and question the quality of his relationships with Tree and Eve. He stood silently pondering and processing over the events which had taken place. Adam was evaluating the value and integrity of his alleged friends uncertain whether to forgive the cast of lowly performers for accepting such demoralizing roles.

Eve could see by the look on Adams face that he was not in a rejoicing or celebratory mood. She delt confined to the narrow and awkward position placed begore her. At the very moment Adam was fed up and wanted nothing more to do with Eden instantly regretting his decision of having ever returned to visit. He now perceived the gardened paradise as nothing more than a troubled body of land that was overly decorated and wildly pollenated. Eden seemed nothing more to than an elaborately designed circuit of shrubs intended to mislead and deceive its inhabitants.

Adam was uncomfortable with the thought of leaving Eve to care for their child alone. He understood that Eve's lack of maternal experience would ultimately force her to call on God for aide and support. Adams fiery temper and bruised ego refused to allow God the satisfaction of rearing his child. Gods' constant pursuit and ongoing failed attempts to repossess Adam was now being waged against the next generation his offsprings. The thought of an unruly and absent king claiming ownership and dominion over his creation did not sit well with Adam. The very idea seemed to infringe on the guidelines of spiritual law. The lack of Gods adherence and regard for celestial proprietorship seemed to upset and annoy Adam seeing that he was directly responsible in the conception and creation of this new life.

There exist within the fabric of man an inexplicable trait which is sowed deep within the composition and framework of the beings that makes them uniquely different from other species. This docile and innate gift of love and connection when cultivated helped to flourish and develop into a divine sense to love. The precious mineral serves to protect and contain what they deem to be sacred and dear to them. Eve nursed feelings of disgrace and humiliation after facing the full brunt of Adam's anguish and frustration. She had never experienced the weight of dishonor and embarrassment while in Adams presence and company. His intense and fiery gaze only helped to demonstrate the despair and disappointment felt at having been hoodwinked and deceived by his dearest and closest friends.

Eve at the very moment was certain that Adam despised her now more than ever. She retained a lowly sense of self-worth and began to accept the silent ridicule of berating glare. Eve was emotionally distraught feeling as though she deserved nothing less than Adams unbridled anguish. Her frail heart ached over the looming notion surrounding the possible rekindling of their friendship and bond. Eve desired emotional reconciliation to help restore the tarnished friendship to its original state. She drifted back to a time when admiration and affection flourished between the two friends. The nuptial era of their relationship was absent of tension and awkwardness void of conflict and misunderstandings. Eve felt disorganized more than ever attempting to process the multitude of surging emotions. She was troubled by the unbearable weight of emotional despair. Eve felt damaged and downtrodden, she struggled internally against the feelings of defeat and disappointment. Eve began to forge a barrier of immunity and defense in response to Adams displaced frustration. She began to resolve in her heart and mind that Adam was more upset and bothered by his own moral flawing and recklessness than by the bountiful news of her bearing.

Under the immense pressure anxiety and frustration Eve exploded suddenly without warning. "Go then!" She lashed out at Adam. "Leave if you must!" Eve firmly encouraged. "Do not let this predicament ensnare or keep you here when clearly you do not wish to stay. Run home to you family. Forget this paradise for your own sake for nothing would bring our master more joy than to delay your retreat. If you do not leave than Gods plan will be successful, and our lord and master will be triumphant. Trees life and sacrifice will have been all in vain," Eve paused as if afflicted and grieved by thought and mention of Tree's name.

"Go on and leave." Eve yelled out repeatedly at Adam. "Live free with your family and be merry for rest of your days." Eve began to sulk uncontrollably attempting to contain the puddle of tears streaming down her nimble face, "I wanted you to be mine." Eve cried out. "But not like this, not under these circumstances, and certainly not because of a child!" An awkward moment of silence fell over the two. The air of silence and discomfort would have lingered further had it not been for Eve's interjection. "Since our introduction, I have found myself irritably engrossed by you," Eve confessed openly to Adam. "But to my discovery and misfortune, I could not have you for myself. At the time as you were happily committed and holding firm to the boundaries of your relationship. Your inaccessibility should have served as a deterrent but instead it filled me contempt and jealousy. I was confronted with the irrefutable fact that I could not make you mine." Eve unfurled her feelings openly refusing to hold back any longer. "The feeling and affection I held for you burned deep within me like a fiery flame filling my frigid body and heart with warmth. I intended to uphold and honor the boundaries of our friendship, but it appeared that I was only deceiving myself. I attempted to disenchant myself by minimizing my fascination and infatuation for you. However, restraining my attraction for you was not within the scope of my will or self-control. I was naive to believe that I could somehow control the wave of intense emotions without allowing it to engulf me. Upon Tree's admission and my own exploration and discovery I have come to understand that my attraction and feelings for you were predetermined as part of Gods conceptual plan. However, at this moment as I stand before you uncertain and in question as to my regard and affection for you. I come to question whether the fondness and admiration I reserve for you are my own natural inclinations. Or are they simply instinctual flaws embedded deep withing the makeup of my design."

The thought of being used as pawn and manipulated by God seemed to greatly distress and trouble Eve. "Please believe me Adam," Eve implored. "When I discovered that my purpose and existence was to serve as tool of seduction in your ensnarement made me truly unsettled. The burden of my troubles only increased after I was made aware by Tree that the debt of my life and existence was owed to your partner and mate." "Wait," Adam interrupted. "How long have you been aware of this?" He demanded in a stern and firm tone. "I have known for some time," Eve answered piteously. "However, not before the day of our consummation. Please allow me to explain." Eve begged sobbing woefully.

"God appeared shortly after your departure very much angry and filled with rage. He suggested that somehow Tree and I were the reason and cause for your abrupt departure and extended absence. God punished Tree severely for her treason by painfully uprooting her from the ground. As for myself I was mistreated and scolded harshly. God berated me reminding of my lowly station and of my single purpose and use to him. He cursed the gift of freewill and threatened to never create another creature that he could not oppress or control directly. God anticipated your return to Eden relying on the emotional connection and affection your reserve for Tree. God assured your untimely return and groomed me with the offer of your fidelity, and love as my reward if I supported his endeavor. He offered to provide me a new muse and object of affection. God aims to resurrect his failed ambitions by replacing you with another life to serve and reign in your place as his prince and herald. I accepted the confidential role being offered and recruited myself in the colluding and conspiring of your entrapment. I was then provided with specific details and instructions on how I was to proceed. It shames me to have to bring into question our courtship or to have you look on at me distastefully for having fulfilled the obligations shortly after."

Adam stood frozen in silence and consumed with disgust. His hands caressed the creases on his forehead perplexed and somewhat bewildered. "Do you recall that fateful night?" Eve asked in gentle and soft tone. "When we first laid together beneath the sycamore trees, away from the prying eyes of the forest. We drew our fingers through the night sky to connect the gleaming stars. That was the night you confessed your love openly in exchange for my virtue. I see now that it was silly of me to assume that your admission of love was genuine and not sourced from lustful desires. I am sorry Adam," Eve pleaded, "Tree tried to warn me of our king's cunning and craftiness, but I failed miserably to heed her warnings."

Adam rested his head between his palms as though burdened with shame and guilt. He felt entangled by the very feelings Eve was attempting to evoke. A whirlwind of emotions began to surface through Adams body as his mind began to spiral with unsavory thoughts. The caracol of images and memories that gathered in his mind spun like moving pictures. Adam recounted his final moments with Tree reflecting on their relationship with empathic lenses. He began to understand and appreciate the great lengths and risks in which she undertook to assure his safety and protection. Adam began to piece together the clues and crumbs left by Tree cautioning him against the craftiness and shrewdness of their astute king. Adam began to stitch and weave observations and patterns reasons as to why Tree chose not to speak so candidly whenever in Eve's presence. Adam was consumed with defeat, frustration and confusion. He found himself heavily wrought between the coils of surmountable pain and disappointment. The impact of his betrayal seemed to collapse the universe around him.

Adam had yet to accept the loss of his dear friend despite being given little time to cope or process his grief. An eruption of emotions ignited his senses exposing him to an array of uncomfortable feelings. Upset and outraged Adam expressed his discontent with flagrance and vulgar disappointment etched in his tone. His childish rage and bouts of untamed frustration resembled an emotional tantrum that would subside and eventually wane slowly over time. Adam realized that his childish behavior would not change or affect the inevitable fate of his dueling circumstances. He fell into state of acute depression and briefly entertained the idea and thought of consolidating his losses and depart from Eden and never return. Adam was unable to cope with the thought of abandoning Eve in her dire time of need and instinctively assumed the port and position of provider and protector. In those few silent moments Adam imagined every possible outcome involving his absence. None moved him more than the thought and image of his bastard child raising his arms cursing the name of his father for having forsaken and denied involvement in his life.

Adam slowly moved his face away from his hands face exposing the warm dew of tears drenched in his palms. Viewing Adam's dampened face and drooling eyes Eve felt helpless and was once again overcome with sorrow and grief. She disrobed her silent and callous demeanor with a whimpering outcry as she ran to Adam collapsing piteously into his arms. Adam held Eve together firmly fastened in his grips unable to release his hold or pull himself away from her. Adam struggled internally with his emotions feeling powerless by Eve's touch scarcely able to escape the allure of her sensual gaze. Eve was tenderly moved and somewhat surprised by Adam's sudden offer to postpone and reconsider his imminent departure and retreat from Eden.

Eves eyes relayed the message of mutual sentiments although affectionately unspoken. Adam wrestled with many indecision's and shuttered at the thought of betraying his mate, and family once again. He could feel the dampening warmth of Eve's face coiled against the bridge of his shoulder. Adam began to drift seamlessly beneath the quilted comforts of his own mind. He pondered with overwhelming strain over the severity and weight of his current dilemma and circumstances. Feeling bested and outwitted Adam was left with no other means or method of resolve then to produce except a silent and whimpering outcry. His salty tears traveled down the path his lean face before breaching the bridge of his chin. Moist drops began to spill over Eve's neck and backside. Adam held tightly to Eve nestling the creature dangerously close to his chest and body. The tenderness of Eve's touch seemed to remove the deep stain of resentment and contempt that Adam presently harbored. In the silence of the night beneath the vast breadth of the glimmering stars the odd pairing found themselves comforting one another beneath an outpouring of muffled whimpers their sorrowful tears.

4

The Entanglement

Adam concluded his meeting with Eve and set forth on his departure home. He tarried about wandering aimlessly through Eden in deep thought. Adam was nervous and somewhat anxious about the idea of returning home. In his mind he dreaded the jarring encounter and was not looking forward to having to disclose the kept secret. "How can I explain to my partner and son." Adam thought, "and expect them not to detest and scorn me for of my betrayal." The fog of uncertainty that covered his mind seemed to also cloud his sense of judgment.

The weight of Adams troubles burdened him deeply observed by his slow and lethargic demeanor. Adam paced in weary manner moving sluggishly through the garden. He moved as though the ground was paved in sticky black tar clinging to his feet. Every step forward seemed like a chore for Adam completed begrudgingly. His thoughts roamed free and untamed as he recounted the events of the day. Adam rehashed the past cursing his earthly limitations with the inability to manipulate or reverse time. He felt cursed and luck ridden very much deprived of options. Adam fell to his knees and clasped his hands together and began to chant and pray. Feeling hopelessly inept Adam began to question his ability to endure and balance two homes and manage two families. The divisive lifestyle soon became an overwhelming thought for Adam. "It is simply impossible." Adam grieved out loud. "How can I be expected to exist in two places at

44

once?" He pondered heavily for some time over the flawed concept and after finding no plausible answers to his dilemma he concluded his efforts. Left with no other means of support Adam called out to this father and creator, acknowledging the very mastermind and architect of his troubles and undoing. Adam humbly knelt and clutched his hands against his chest he began praying.

"God," Adam called out. "I pray that you reveal yourself to me." He demanded in a proud and unabashed voice. However, God did not answer his call. "I know you hear me father, I know that you look down on me glaringly, mocking my every gesture. You hide your face behind the soft clouds of heaven enjoying a carefree life of luxury and high reverence. You look down on us like insignificant ants struggling to survive. How does a father justify turning away his face and ignoring the pouring outcry for support and assistance from his son." Adam suddenly broke into tears. "You are my father!" Adam poured out openly. "However, you behave as though you are my opposition and competitor. You seem to scoff at my triumphs and achievements and rejoice over my tribulations and woes. All this because of I refuse to surrender my will and abandon my family."

"I did not deserve to endure the harsh treatment your warrantless neglect." Adam stated wholeheartedly. "And still, you taunt me to this day without discretion or reservation. You look to ridicule my every decision with your indignant laughter fully committed to the relinquishment of my joy. You seek to disrupt the peace and solace which I accrued in my life and replace it with chaos, and discord. I can no longer recall the hubris offence I committed to deserve such disdain and abuse. It appears that I am entirely void of your blessing and generosity. Well, no more! Tonight, with the stars as my witness, I call out to you to make amends for my trespassing's and plead for your mercy and forgiveness." Adam was overcome by the humbling spirit of harmony to offer an apology and make amends with his father, and someway ask for forgiveness.

"I kneel before you today father," Adam cried out. "Offering my surrender at the heels of your pursuit. I pray you allow me to purge the blemish of disdain from my sullied name. I never intended to challenge or defy your supreme authority, but only reacted in defense of my values doing what I felt was just. I see now the weight of my decision, and how my choosing another over you can been deemed offensive. I stumbled onto companionship and discovered a different form of love, one that would ultimately propel me to the brinks of fatherhood. I have come to enjoy the pleasures of domestication and wish for nothing more than to experience eternity alongside my newly formed family. I proudly accepted the paternal role with a noble sense of purpose. I drew strength confidence in my ability to fulfill the role of provider and protector of my family and home. I managed to assure the welfare and safety of my family by navigating them through the unpredictable and treacherous terrains of everyday life. The trails of fatherhood can be a deflating and humbling experience however filled monumental moment of great joy."

Adam paused for a moment uncertain whether to continue with his lengthy passioned filled prayer. The silent reception of unrequitedness only helped to further irritate and provoke Adam. His fiery temper seemed to fuel the growing resentment he harbored at having submitted to prayer. The highly volatile and explosive emotions which Adam kept bottled up and suppressed were presently being uncorked by the hands of ignorance and arrogance. Adam was insightful in recognizing that his pent-up emotions were purposeless in garnering support for his plea. In collecting his composure Adam was able to subdue and confront the negative feelings before losing his temper. "I have come to accept the false narrative of your absence as my truth," Adam spoke emphatically. "When I was young, I made reasonable accommodations for your absenteeism and extended vacancy in my life. I found comfort in believing that your celestial occupation drew you away from Eden and away from me. I could only imagine the weight of responsibility it took to uphold and maintain order in the universe.

I grew up accepting that the magnitude of your vocation did not afford you the luxury of being present or active in life. But when you appeared to me in the garden I was estranged and somewhat shocked by the sudden introduction. The mutual sense of estrangement between us produced an emotional rift which in my opinion may have been severed during my early development." Adam could hear himself rambling cathartically finding solace and clarity in his speech.

"I bear no ill will or animosity regarding my removal and banishment from my garden. Though, I still hold the firm conviction and belief that I could have benefited more from your supervision and interaction then from your absence and neglect. When you never came, I began to foster feelings of resentment and bitterness towards you. I removed you from my heart and erased you from my thoughts because I did not want to become you. I desired higher aspirations for myself with the intrusive hopes of one day becoming an equally powerful force or possibly even greater than yourself. This mindset has helped me to forge my own path of an architect and creator like yourself. And though I lack the majestic qualities of your godly traits I am endowed with the powers of guardianship serving as protector, and provider."

Adam started to reflect on his relationship with his son and began to project his feelings. "I wanted nothing more than to have a son of my own," Adam scoffed playfully with grin. "A creature I would bathe with attention, and shower with assurances. A creature that I could teach, and mold and provide guidance and mentorship. I would help him to understand that I am his god and creator and that he too ultimately shares the same royal bloodline and lineage. Such a creature would serve as a beacon of light illuminating faith and hope over the darkness and uncertainties of the world. Cain has exceeded my greatest hopes to become the fiery ember that warms my heart. He is dearly coveted and invaluable to my heart. I instilled within Cain the foundational pillars of conventional wisdom. Respect, honor, strength, discipline and most importantly dedication. I bestowed these morals teachings and principals demonstrating the value of universal love for all creations, and to regard and honor his creators especially.

Understand, that Cain is my gift and prize in this world. The laboring of his passage and transition was not easy but rather an excruciating journey. I am forever indebted to my mate for bearing the full grunt and weight of the incredible process. The painful sacrifice demonstrated fortitude and bravery in the face of agonizing turmoil and adversity. It is clear to see that without my mate's assistance and support our child Cain would cease to exist as would my newly formed sense of purpose and pride." Adam inhaled deeply a gust of air into his lungs only to release a sighing breath of exhaustion from his nostrils. "I wished to bestow the one gift I deeply desired and sought after but could not obtain." Adam paused a moment to allow the wave of emotions to subside. "The invaluable gift of my presence was all that I could offer my son as his father. As Cain's creator I wield a sense of dedication and devotion to protect and provide for him. And should he happen to call out to me in his time of need I will be ready to assist and support him. I am prepared as Cain's father to offer direction and guidance in navigating the traitorous terrains of life. It is my duty to minimize the pitfalls and obstacles he will eventually come to face. I realize that all that I ever wanted from my creator was his acknowledgment and support; that is the only decent thing that any father can offer to their child."

"And as I have said before but will repeat once again I have long since forgiven you, and no longer harbor any ill will against you. I was a young then and did not fully comprehend the dynamic complexities of life. But now I stand before you no longer a child but as a man and God in my own respects. Like you, I too have managed to forge and create life, but in the act of tending and caring for my new creation I have discovered and redefined my purpose. The path of my destiny is not defined by who I am but rather what I represent to those that I cherish and hold dear. I have come to view myself through the empathetic eyes and lenses of my adoring family."

"I arrived here today with the intention of visiting my dear friend Tree but was shocked to discover that she has been removed from her post. As you aware Tree is the one with whom I owe abundantly for my rearing, and upbringing. I feel morally obligated to stand before you and plead for her return. Tree is to me the epitome of love serving as the foundational pillars upon which my honor and resilience rest. I plead humbly before you on this day requesting for Trees return and reinstatement. There is no other creature with whom I adore and would willingly lay down my own life in exchange for her safe return. I would surrender my will and kneel before your feet if you accepted my plea to restore and revive Tree. In exchange, I will honor the bulk of my responsibility by nurturing and fathering the child that I have conceived with Eve. I will provide the necessary support in rearing and caring of the highborn. I will demonstrate equal commitment and patience to fulfill my duties and obligation, just as I have with my own son. I will rear the gentle child offering as much tenderness and affection as permeable to my being. However, if you choose to deny my request." Adam declared with a fiery glow over his face. "I will leave Eden and never look back at this place again. I will forever regard this paradise as an estranged and forbidden land. A fertile graveyard housing the bones and remains of severed memories and distant relationships. Eden will become a myth in time and history as I am prepared to deny its very existence in falsehood and promote the unsettling truth. I am ready to abandon this grand estate and depart once and for all if need be. You have successfully managed to tarnish my relationship with Eve by sowing seeds of doubt and mistrust. I do not wish to lose the acquaintance of a dear friend; however, I will leave if I must."

Adam concluded his lengthy speech fully drenched with his face fully immersed in tears. He scarcely noticed the shadowy figure lurking nearby in the foreground amidst the rustling bushes. It was Eve, who had been eavesdropping and overheard the private prayer and confessional. She found herself rather moved and taken aback by the passion filled oath of Adam's pledge. Eve struggled to fight back her tears. She wanted to speak out and offer soothing words of comfort and reassurance to Adam. Eve had witnessed Adam speak passionately and openly regarding his feelings and emotions. His lowly spirits seemingly contemptuous and bruised carried an unsettling odor resembling the scent of defeat. Adam's exodus from Eden was a painful, and mournful thought for Eve to conceive. The very idea of Adam's withdrawal cut deeply like a festering wound over Eve's heart. His conviction and declaration to relinquish his support was rather unsettling. Eve appeared confused by his admission. In her interaction with Adam, she believed that she had already convinced and won his commitment. Eve assumed she that had removed the lingering thread of doubt from the seams of Adam's mind. She believed that she had derailed his plan of self-exile and permanent departure from Eden. She refused to accept Adams declaration and would have denied the report as fictitious and untrue had she not witnessed for herself the remarks made during his prayer. The was an observational distinction between Adam's prayer to God, and that of his private meeting and conversation with Eve.

"I shall return again tomorrow at high noon." Adam stated boldly looking over his shoulders in the direction of the ruffling bushes. Adam caught a glimpse of Eve lurking in the shadows. Adam did not shy away or turn from Eve's gaze but rather he rejoiced in her presence. The declaration of Adam's message had been officially notarized thru Eve's accounting and presence as a witness. Looking at Eves teary eyes and moistened face Adam finalized his ultimatum. "If Tree is restored then I will undoubtedly father my child with Eve declaring the communal path to reconciliation. The unborn child can very well serve as a testimonial symbol of peace and union. The very creature possesses the potential to end our long-standing feud and rivalry." Eve wanted to speak out if nothing more leap out from the behind the bushes and run madly into Adams arms. She wanted desperately to console Adam and serve as a voice of reassurance restoring faith and confidence back into him. Despite her good intention Eve found that she could not move and was held captive by fear and trepidation. Eve could neither find the nerves nor the fortitude to act or speak out cowering within the confines of the floral bush.

"Only after Tree's return will the union and bond between father and son be fully restored. You will forever exist in my good graces just as I will be solemnly secured in yours. I vow before your very name with Eve to serve as our witness. I will be all that I am, and care for the child as of my own flesh and blood. Believe that in my heart nothing would make me happier or bring me more joy than to father our child..." It was at this point that Adam seemed to shift the conversation in the direction towards Eve, who was still within an earshot listening attentively. Her concealed and avoidant behavior mimicked that of her omniscient and powerful master. "I swear by my good name," Adam concluded. "And everything that I hold dear and sacred in this world. I will commit and keep my promise to never return to Eden if your king and master does not fulfill my single unselfish request."

Eve stared at Adam with a paralyzing gaze as though stunned by the clarity of his words. She wrestled with her thoughts and emotions wanting desperately to cry out. Eve wallowed and wailed privately within the secured chambers of her mind. "What of me, and what of us?" She queried privately. "What will become of our love?" Unfortunately, none of these words or thoughts managed to escape her lips. The avid stream of tears that ran down her sunken face spoke volumes to demonstrate the full extent of her pain staked beneath wrenching heartache. "Good-bye, Eve" Adam announced casually, "I truly hope this will not be our final farewell."

Adam turned around slowly and began walking away. Despite the distance between Eve and himself, Adam could still hear her sorrowful outpouring fading in the background. The very sound of her woeful cries was filled with anguish and pain. The sorrowful noise was unbearable for Adam to endure. He painted the final image of Eve hiding in the bushy forest her face soaked with tears. Marked by agonizing betrayal Adam sought to bring an end to the already drawn-out scene. He managed his sorrows by viewing himself objectively like an abstract image inside of a rare and beautiful painting. Adam saw himself withing scaling portrait of his mind walking away off into the distance. Both he and Eve wore looks of hurt and regret across their faces.

The journey to the wall seemed more daunting than usual for Adam as he furthered his way. The weight of his legs felt strangely bulky and stiff and were rather difficult to maneuver. Despite the intense discomfort in his legs Adam was persistent and determined to make his way out of Eden. He ventured aimlessly through the untamed jungle having lost his way twice in ever evolving garden. Adam continued walking until he finally he came across the grand walls far off in the distance. The sight of the grand walls brought Adam great joy as he was beginning to feel entrenched and lost within the perilous maze and labyrinth of Eden. Adam found himself overcome with joy and relief after coming into view of the massive structure a few yards away.

Adam felt revitalized and once again instantly filled with energy and vigor. The bearings of his feet and heels seemed to regain their strength and vitality with Adam moving more agile with every step forward. Adam began to increase his speed by lengthening his stride. The sudden burst of speed seemed to elevate Adams agility as he sprinted across the open plains towards the grand wall. Adam did not stop at the doorway but instead continued his run, passing quickly through the stony corridor and tunneled pathway. He moved swiftly thru to the other side and did not stop running until he was exhausted and out of breath. Adam dropped down to the ground and collapsed suddenly onto his knees seemingly delighted and overcome with relief. He smiled dubiously to himself uncertain whether to rejoice for having made it through to the other side. It was difficult for Adam to express the feeling of relief and comfort that engulfed him after returning home. The desolate and barren wasteland was gradually becoming Adam preferred landscape and environment.

5

The Exchange

The next day Adam returned to the Eden as promised. His journey to the grand wall was filled with tension and anxiety. He begrudgingly entered the paradise drawing little joy over the illustrious garden. The extravagant landscape had somehow lost its wondrous appeal leaving Adam with a host of incorrigible thoughts. "What if Tree has not been returned?" Adam considered the possibility still uncertain the path of recourse he would pursue. "What will I say to Eve." Adam thought. "How will I begin to explain myself." The private narrative and discourse of self-examination plagued Adam on his travels as he furthered deeper into Eden. A chill of nervousness crept through Adam's body moving closer into the sacred vicinity and heart of the garden.

Adam walked into the garden wielding optimism in his heart, while still allowing space for disappointment. He stepped cautiously forward nervous and fearful of what he would uncover. Entering the epicenter of the garden Adam scanned the perimeter of space around him. Adam was confronted and faced with the astonishing surprise to discover his dearest friend Tree, revived and well. Adam instantly drew a breath of relief scarcely able to contain his excitement. Seeing Tree restored in her usual place brought him immense joy filling his spirit with delight. Tree was firmly stationed in her usual post seemingly unfazed and unaffected as if nothing had happened. Her sturdy limbs stretched outward like several arms reaching toward the sun.

The bulk of Tree's branches and boughs scaled upward and swayed back and forth as though waving out to Adam. The encouraging gesture and motion seemed to welcome and invite him for a warm embrace. The bushel of Tree's crown and leafy green hair was conditioned and renewed to a vibrant hue and youthful pigment.

The mass of her body could be observed by the thick bulge of her roots protruding deep beneath the soiled earths. Viewing Tree in her fully formed and developed state brought a sense of satisfaction to Adam. He was very much pleased to find his dearest friend planted firmly beneath the rays of the glowing sun. It would be difficult for anyone to assume that Tree was indeed the eldest of all the Gods creations. Tree was undoubtedly one of Gods most invaluable creations considering her utility and usefulness in permeating the fabric of nature. Her very existence served as a gift to this world allowing for the preservation and sustainment of nearly every creature to proceed and come after. Adam was glad to find that his wise and faithful matriarch had been fully redeemed to her noble place at the center of the garden. Her youthful posture stood fully erect and upright to compliment her somewhat vigorous and rejuvenated figure. Tree's renewed appearance looked refreshingly vibrant, and radiantly flawless after obtaining God's mercy and grace as well as his restoration.

Her bushy leafy hair was abundant and full covering most of her face. Green vines draped down over Trees shoulders and down her back. The rich texture of hair was well-nourished and parted neatly braided in the most unusual fashion. The thicket of long slender stems that draped and dressed Tree reminded Adam of his childhood. He reminisced over past times when he as a child would grapple and swing happily from vine to vine beneath the base of Trees canopy. Adam recalled how much heftier and thicker the vines seemed in those younger years.

Tree looked simply ravishing she appeared nothing like the gruesome image that Adam carried from his horrid dreams. He unwillingly recalled the troubling image of Tree from his nightmares and quickly became tense made uneasy. The very thought alone reflecting on his dreams began to fill his soul with depression and despair but luckily for Adam he was not dreaming. At present good fortune and favor seem to prevail outside his imagination over the earthly realm. Tree looked healthy and well standing beneath the clear blue skies. She looked more radiant and beautiful than he had ever seen her. The deep hue of green exposed a youthful ambiance over her appearance. Her enriched brown skin shone flawlessly shimmering against the sunlight. Tree glowed radiantly with little effort it was safe to assume that the restorative treatment would be more than enough to sustain her for several centuries. The celestial makeover was a major improvement that helped to enhance Tree's outer image and allowed her to retain her rank and natural position as Eden's most prominent and dignified elder.

Adam could scarcely recognize Tree in her newly refined design and somewhat enhanced form. He moved closer to have a better look at his dear friend. Adam intended to greet and welcome Tree back to Eden however as drew closer he was riddled with shock and surprise to find her in the company and presence of Eve. Eve was asleep resting peacefully at the time of Adams arrival and did not stir or awaken. Eve was lying slumped against the large base of Tree's trunk.

Adam would later come to learn through by Tree's admission that Eve spent most of the early parts of day tending and caring for her needs. Eve helped Tree to reacclimate back into Eden by providing debriefings and updates. She offered detailed summary of all that had transpired during the duration of her absence. Tree listened closely to Eves retelling with glowing suspense and unparalleled astonishment over all that had transpired. The feelings of pride and love which she kept reserved began to surface. The fiery embers of her admiration burned brighter and more intensely after learning of Adams valiant ultimatum, and proposition to resolve the dilemma. "Adam was simply amazing." Eve declared in her retelling. "He stood before God, and demanded your safe return and passage, vowing to never return back Eden if you were not restored."

Eve did not want to endure the pain, and heartbreak that would entail after Adam's absolute absence. In Eve's retelling of the occurrence, she omitted the fact that she too had pleaded with the king to bring Tree back for the sake of retaining Adam in the kingdom. Eve did not wish to see Adam depart from Eden leaving her to nurse and rear their child alone.

Eve submitted her appeal shortly after Adams departure while beneath the weight of grief and sorrow. She demonstrated her submission to God by kneeling to pray. "My lord, king and creator I kneel before you as your loyal, and faithful servant. I am but a simple cog in your ingenious and grand scheme as you are the masterful architect. I have no intent to question your will or test your patience. However, I find myself flawed and uneasy at the present dilemma and the unraveling of my destiny. If you allow Adam to leave and never return, then I will be forever undone. The contents of my heart feel empty and hollow as I find myself overwhelmed with grief. I cannot say that I am satisfied with having loved and lost such a dear acquaintance as Adam. The very intention of my existence seems flawed and meaningless in his absence," Eve began to unpack her the baggage of her emotions before the king., "I feel sorrowful and without any purpose." She pleaded, "I question whether I alone can rear this child and assume both parental roles. The thought and idea of raising a child by herself left Eve feeling somewhat uneasy and tense."

"I am expected to bear and carry into this world another being and creation to serve your biding and complete your plan. But tell me father, what precious values am I expected to instill into the precious offspring if I am left to rear the child alone. Adam has captured my heart, and affection. At this moment I account that he still retains my love. I am aware that I fall short in obtaining his requited and complete adoration, but still the small portion of affection that I receive; whenever I look into his eyes is more than enough to justify my pursuit and purpose. I only wish to bring good fortune and bestow everlasting happiness over Adam. It is to him that I owe the transactional generosity of my life and existence. It was Adam, who helped to bring me to life by providing you with a locket of his partners hair." Eve dispelled intricate details in her master plan and scheme She revealed truths and secrets which were not originally intended for her level of access and exposure.

"Tree raised Adam." Eve declared candidly. "She supported and mothered him. A large portion of respect and honor is notably due for her sacrifice. I believe that she would be a fantastic matron and guide for me. Tree can serve as a midwife and sponsor teaching me all the priceless values of motherhood. I can think of no other creature more suitable to support in the tending and rearing my child. Together Tree and I will instill within the child your benevolent values in allegiance with your ambition." Eve paused for a short moment. "I wish to multiply." She confessed bluntly. "And give life to countless souls that will faithfully serve at your feet and march at your will. But I cannot do it alone." Eve expressed with submission in her tone. "I beg that you pardon Adams ill-tempered declarations and make allowance for his single request. Please return Tree back to him so that he can remain in Eden and fulfill his destiny."

The king had not spoken or responded to either of their calls however the sentiments of their pleading outcries had not fallen on deaf ears. God was neither moved nor was he touched by the opinions and prayers of his delinquent creations. God was beginning to view the entire ordeal and creation of man as a toilsome and increasingly burdensome task. The small fragment of patience and compassion he reserved for his beloved creations was beginning to diminish and dwindle. The king listened to the bulk of Adam and Eve's complaints and grievances cloaked and disguised as prayers. As God listened on to their pleas and outcries, he found himself confronted with the overwhelming truth that his creations were riddled with fear and trepidation. The seed of remorse began to unfurl and grow into shame and guilt as God replayed over in his mind the context and content or their remarks. God sat stoically gazing away into the furthest realms of the universe. The king felt confronted and somewhat uneasy with the unsettling feeling as though he was being ransomed and dictated by his own creations.

God contemplated for some time as to the appropriate response and course of action. The king found himself second guessing the sovereignty of his own power in having to manage and account for the misguidance of his subordinates. He conjured shadowy images in his mind of Adam fulfilling his promise and threat of his succession. God foresaw with omnipotent precision the cascading avalanche of events that would take place once Adam departed Eden for good. Gods' insight and omniscient ability to peer into the future allowed him to observe firsthand the grim fate of humanity. The conclusion of Gods premonition was contingent solely on Adam's absence as opposed to the outcome and possibilities of his retention. He pondered intensely staring off into the furthest distance of space beyond the celestial cluster of stars and swirling planets. God began to envision and imagine a world that would eventually come to pass. "I foresee a chaotic and uncivil world void of order and structure." God casually propelled thru time projected through a carousel of images. He skimmed through centuries and millenniums of man's descent and plight marveling shamefully over all that he saw. God was able to monitor a multitude of endless possibilities and variable outcomes. He was able to foreshadow the inevitable fall and demise and of his creations. God scoured through various realms and dimensions in search of an alternative outcome and conclusion to of his masterful plan. It was inevitable to deny that his plans would be foiled and made stagnant by Adam's radical declaration of self-removal.

The very virtue and fate of man seemed to be at jeopardy with growing tension between God and his creatures. He watched through sharp rapid images the rapid degradation and decline of his creations over time. The visions began to grow increasingly more troublesome as he imagined two worlds existing congruent of the other. The geography of one world was well preserved and gorgeously arranged. The land was considerably lavish and abundant with goods and livestock. The inhabitants of this bountiful world appeared to be well off and were afforded access to luxuries inherited by those born and housed within the comfort and confines of Eden's borders. The vision brought a smile over the king's face at seeing the massive demonstration of creatures roaming aimlessly and carefree about the land. The children and descendants of Eve had generationally aged and were now garnering offspring of their own. The citizens of Eden were comfortable and content living within civil caste system based off class and privilege. The peaceful civilization existed untroubled and unfazed by the paradoxical world that existed beyond their neighboring wall. The inhabitants of Eden were encouraged to stay away from the grand walls. They were instructed to exercise caution and to never interfere or interact with the inhabitants and those on other side of the wall.

God shifted his attention from Eden to the barren and grim world beyond the grand walls. God was neither shocked nor surprised to discover the massive number of beings inhabiting the land. The creatures were undoubtedly the children and descendants of Adam. The census of his offsprings predominantly outnumbered the population of creatures residing within Eden. The untamed seedlings of Adam's royal lineage seemed to sow the earth freely. They carried little regard for moderation and even less value in resources. Unlike their counterparts in Eden the outsiders held separate and unique ideologies. They accepted the existential propaganda that dictated the genesis of their lineage and existence. Adams descendants would learn to perverse the doctrines of freedom to honor the legacy of their patron. Adam's protest and refusal to submit before the highest power was truly an inspiring narrative that the people of the wastelands accepted and carried with pride. The defiant spirit of their ancestor seemed to be embedded within fabric and spirit of his descendants. His royal lineage retained an entitled sense of pride and esteem over their survival and mastery of the wild lands. Adam's descendants were uncouth and spiritually decayed by earthly standards. The nomadic outcast could easily be observed as insatiable in their diet and appetite. They appeared to be pitiful and misguided creatures lacking the spiritual protein and moral fiber of godliness. Adam's children ran amuck conquering large quantities of the vast lands. They demolished and stripped away at the land removing any trace of existence. They hunted and killed off massive numbers the wild beasts that grazed and roamed the wild lands.

Adam's unruly offspring were less inclined to submit or accept the idea of an omnipotent king ruling over them. The nation of misguided souls appeared vaguely unfamiliar and detached from the origins of their royal heritage and lineage. The outsiders banned together in collective consciousness in denial of their sacred connection to God. They neither worshiped nor praised their noble king despite sharing a sacred bond. Like lambs led astray down the dark pasture of wicked intent so were these lost souls and spirits squandering carelessly over the lands. Disorder, and chaos seemed to reign over the world before him. The children and descendants of Adam did not know the name of their omnipotent creator nor did the creatures care to learn his name or show interest. In their eyes God was nothing more than a fable that lived in the mind and hearts of little children. They repudiated the omniscient king with condemning disregard. The creatures were unwilling to accept God as their master and ruler. God was deeply saddened and fraught with disappointment to discover that Adam had not passed down the legacy of his ancestry to his descendants. However, the truth of the matter was that Adam had little reason to mention or teach his children about the existence of an omniscient and neglectful God. One who regarded himself as the supreme patriarch and source of all existence.

Speeding quickly through time God came to view his wonderful paradise in utter ruins. The impenetrable grand fortress that separated Eden from the outside world had been demolished and was now overtaken by rouge tyrants and vigilantes. Adam descendants managed to invade Eden transforming the beautiful oasis into a barren and tarnished wasteland. The destruction of the grand wall served to signify a change in the trajectory of human history. The demolition of the grand wall resulted in a large migration of Adams descendants crossing into Eden. They colonized and claimed Eden as their homeland belonging rightfully to their great ancestor Adam. The large influx of creatures coming into Eden caused a surplus in population which resulted in. a food shortage. Eden eventually fell into crises faced with scarcity of goods and resources. The savage newcomers pillaged and desecrated the garden hunting down as many creatures and animals as they saw fit. The wild untamed brutes as God considered them were relentless in their siege and conquest of Eden. The parasitic miscreants seemed only to be interested in removing and erasing the beauty and bounty that was once Eden. Impudent and bold were Adams descendants oblivious and unlearned creatures sadly primitive and unaware of the fearful wrath and fury of their omnipotent creator and landlord. The common practice of willful ignorance towards their God and master greatly devalued the worth and equity of their souls. Adams descendants were spiritually frugal and morally bankrupt offering little value to name of their king. They constantly quarreled and bickered amongst with one another. These quarrels would eventually develop into contentious rivalries which over centuries set the frontier for battles and wars to be waged. The descendants who now occupied Eden lived in division rather than unity as their predecessors. They created feudal caste systems which thrived heavily on the oppression and subjugation of others through forced slavery and indentured work and labor. The new residents and inhabitants of the garden would eventually find themselves being consumed by ignorance and seduced by greed. The unsanctioned integration of Eden now housed a magnitude of lustful sinners and influencers determined to distract the citizens from the greatness of purpose their and design.

To gain more clarity and understanding of the dire circumstances being staged before him the king dialed back the hands of time. He was determined to view the precipitating events which led to his undoing. God watched on as Adam's children multiplied growing vast in numbers with each passing generation. Adam's offspring produced a higher frequency of souls into the world increasing the sum of their physical presence. It was only a matter of time before Adam's children would begin their endless crusade to charter and explore the deserted and barren wastelands. Their voyage eventually brought them further into the region's and paramotors of the grand walls. His descendants would eventually come to discover the monumental barricade and vast barrier that was the grand wall. At first the wall served its purpose in keeping outsiders from entering Eden. They marveled over the strange and mysterious wall made entirely granite and mortar. The largely erect wall served as a boarder and divider separating the two worlds. The grand wall was useful in providing comfort and protection to the inhabitants inside the beautiful paradise but did very little to accommodate those on the other side of the boarder. Inevitably it would be man's curiosity and insatiable appetite for knowledge and truth that would become his undoing. Despite being faced with the gospel of truth Adam's children and descendants refused to be accept that the same supernatural force responsible for forming the moon and the cosmos also built the wall around them. The invaders used primitive weapons and tools to chip away at the exterior and outer layering of the massive wall. The daunting undertaking of penetrating the grand wall was not an easy feat to accomplish. It took them nearly two decades to effectively falter and break thru the grand wall. The crumbling wall would eventually reveal a coin sized hole that provided the outsiders a glimpse into the glorious paradise. They rejoiced at having discovered a defenseless world filled with bountiful resources and treasures susceptible to foreign invasion.

God witnessed the demise and destruction of Eden before his very eyes. The wonderful and glorious paradise he spent centuries fostering was now gone. The desperate invaders ransacked Eden stripping the land of all its natural wealth and precious resources. These ill-willed and selfish invaders would eventually come to destroy the garden removing from the sacred lands its beauty and enchantment. The descendants of Adam were unapologetic and low bred creatures. They hunted ravishingly by way of capturing and ensnaring many of the locals living and residing in Eden. The term barbarians were best used to describe the invaders who slew and killed off several inhabitants. They killed both man and mammal; anyone that dared to resist or fight back against their brutish and tactless invasion. God watched helplessly as the animals with whom he crafted through engineering and hard work being slaughtered and killed off like cattle. The genocide and extinction of God's finest and rarest creations was truly an unsettling sight to behold. The few inhabitants and animals that remained were held captive and fastened with harnesses and chains. The were made captive and then domesticated overtime to serve as subjects and tools for their oppressors. The mammals were used for the sole purpose of servicing and aiding man as deemed fit. The four-legged creatures were useful in their ability to transport goods back and forth; however, the degrading cycle of abuse was ultimately frowned upon. The mammals and animals of the began to feel like second rate species and subordinates of man. The botanical paradise which once catalogued and housed the rarest collection of the God's greatest body of works were now being plundered and deflowered from its roots. The thriving agriculture of vegetation and wild fruits which flourished bountifully in Eden was destroyed and uprooted. Eden was in utter ruins as the descendants of Adam had brought chaos and destruction with them in their conquest. It was a sad mournful end to the fanciful paradise that fostered an impressive gallery and collection of Gods greatest and masterful works.

After witnessing these disturbing images and envisioning a future so bleak and grim God grew somewhat saddened if not disappointed by the inevitable outcome of his creation. The fate of man brought with it an unsurmountable air of melancholy grief over the king. The feelings of sorrow mixed with anguish dampened God's mood as he was forced to bear witness to the destruction of his most sacred paradise. Seeing his precious creations being slaughtered and slain senselessly was an unsettling image. Eden appeared utterly dysfunctional and plagued by death, the land was absent in compassion and bankrupt of love. Their world exposed hidden skeletons and bones protruding beneath the sacred earth. The countless lives lost during the battle of Eden would transform the wonderful paradise into a graveyard no different from a cemetery.

The king was filled with deep sadness reflecting considerably on the effort and span of time that it took him to design Eden. God wallowed silently watching as his ambitions and hard work crumble and collapse before his very eyes. The garden that he worked and toiled to help transform into a luxurious paradise was now being sieged by the hands of invaders. At present God felt afflicted and low in spirit. The unpleasant taste of defeat was a bitter and strangely unfamiliar flavor for the king to ingest. God was not accustomed to disappointment and did not enjoy the experience of not having his way. He had lost the spiritual war waged against the powers of evil and was unsettled by the outcome. Anger and rage consumed the king filling his spirit with bitterness and resentment. "Evil shall never prosper!" God exclaimed proudly slamming his fist against the arm of his throne. He refused to allow evil the chance and opportunity to triumph and overthrow his sacred garden. In his blind state of rage and fury God resolved to destroy the world and begin anew. God was prepared to draw from a blank slate and canvas. However, the thought of destruction festered in his mind. The daunting task of recreating another paradise resembling Eden would be incredibly time consuming and over overwhelming. God began to reconsider Adam's request and prayer with celestial insight and spiritual understanding. He viewed Adam as the catalyst that would impact and change the foreseeable outcome of the future. God began to give sound consideration to

Adam's unorthodox appeal to restore and bring Trees back to life. Her resurrection would be crucial to avoid the grim and unfortunate fate that awaited if he denied and dismissed the request.

God understood that without an army of loyal followers, evil would engulf and consume the world. The haunting realization left the king paralyzed in deep thought. God considered the life span and expiration of Adams corrupt descendants. Their earthly transition and spiritual ascension into heaven was a source of strife and great concern for God. The thought of countless souls attempting to breach the fortified gates of heaven was an unsettling thought for the king to conceive. God saw Adams descendent piled together in groves attempting to usurp the reigns of heaven. They were the most wicked and vile spirits attempting to dismantle and unbar the pearly gates. God soberingly accepted the magnitude of his present dilemma. He came to the humbling realization that if left unchecked there would be a massive migration of entitled souls in violent petition to gain access and entry into heaven. God watched as the souls of Adams descendants lingeried and loitered before the heavenly entrance. An insurrection would eventually form over the population of intolerant outcasts. They grew tired and impatient of the bureaucratic system of heavenly policies and began to work together to push and pull-down heavens gates to force their way into eternity. The conquest resembled the overthrowing of the grand wall. Those unkempt and unscrupulous souls still carried mischief and malice in their hearts. They managed to retain the earthly qualities of sin demonstrated in their conduct and behavior. "Those contemptuous souls!" God aguishly remarked "They will ban together in commitment to penetrate my defenses. They look to demolish and my kingdom and fortress just as they have destroyed my paradise on earth. The fate of man now seemed minor and trivial when juxtaposed with the potential fate of heaven. The outcome and result of the feuding war between good and evil was now contingent on a single mortal request. There was only one logical choice to made that would ease the growing hostility and tension looming in the king's heart. Gods' decision was not met without anguish and irritation for allowing himself to put in such a compromising position.

God settled on the matter and was prepared to fulfill Adam's adamant request for Tree's return and reinstatement. The phenomenal powers used to conjure Tree's removal and discharge from the garden was replicated in her restoration. Tree was reinstated and placed back into the plot and fertile mirth of land at the very center and heart of Eden. Tree had been resurrected and peacefully returned from the nether regions. Her undisturbed demeanor disguised any visible signs of abuse or maltreatment. Tree's valiant restoration and return was considered by Eve to be a favorable blessing bestowed in her favor. Eve was convinced in the belief that her pouring outcries had somehow moved the king to commit the kind act. Adam assumed similarly with the same unyielding conviction that it was his plea and desperate prayers that moved God to return his dear friend. God did not feel the need to explain the path of his rational to his subjects. He neither felt the need to justify or account for his actions as to why he chose to return Tree back to them.

Adam and Eve were ignorant of the path to God's deductions however, neither dared to question or explore the true intent and reasoning behind their king's motive. The two would live on with bewildering assumption that it was their personal and private speech that moved their king. God saw no harm in allowing each party to assume that their passion filled declarations and persuasive recommendations resulted in Tree's triumphant return. Neither Adam nor Eve thought to consider the full breadth and weight of their request. Blinded and somewhat misconstrued by their negotiating power the two could not foresee how deeply woven and enmeshed they were at the seams. The private prayers and promises offered by Adam and Eve in exchange for Tree return seemed altruistic, and selfless however the scrupulous terms were steep. Adam and Eve had openly committed themselves before God, keeping the contractual obligations and prayers made during their beseeching prayers. The two advocates willfully accepted their king's judgement and ruling with dignity and honor. The unexplored concept of collaborative parenting was a new and unfamiliar concept. The arena of shared custody was an uncharted and unfamiliar territory for Adam and Eve. However, they agreed to share responsibility for the new creature with neither one daring to diverge or break away from the solemn promise. Adam agreed to carry the weight of his custodial obligations and duties with dignified pride. He endorsed the lifelong assignment with little to no petition. He did not consider the monumental weight and severity of od such a rash and hasty decision. Adam appeared willfully ignorant to the fact that accepting the partnering role of nurturer would ultimately couple and bind him to Eve forever. Consumed with ego and pride Adam somehow believed that he could face the unforeseeable challenge before him and overcome the hurdles of managing two homes. The misguided thought would ultimately extend the boundaries of his relationship and to form and create multiple houses. Adams believed that the sacrifice was necessary for the sake of the greater good. He maintained this mindset all while keeping his word to Eve as they both now shared a mutual interest.

They praised their master, and spoke highly of their merciful king, Adam and Eve chanted and sung songs declaring their unyielding gratitude and allegiance to God. Though the performance was rather endearing God was not fully convinced by pledging act. "The stake and price of loyalty is taxing." God spoke softly. "However, the expense and toll of commitment fetches a hefty sum." And without another word uttered God brought Tree back to life and returned her to rightful place. It was on this faithful night that man first learned to accept the sacred powers of their prayers. Adam retained the knowledge and belief that any obstacle or barrier could by removed with the simple act of prayer. At the time praying and calling out to God was the only feasible channel and path to the king. Prayers were believed to be carried off and delivered through the mythical frequency and powers of alchemy. This was the way God received his direct messages from his followers and constituents.

Consequentially the act of praying required total submission of ones will and unparalleled devotion. The surrender of autonomy ultimately placed the those that praised vulnerable as pray in sense of the word. The contractual prayer often imposed the implication which offered allegiance and favor to God. It was strategic on the part of the king to conceive a pragmatic means of retaining the descendants of Adam within Eden opposed to the other side. In exchange for complete surrender and renouncement God was willing to offer any creature the full scale and bounty of their prayers. He offered to issue allowances for any being willing to surrender their will and accept him as their king and master. In return his followers received the deeds to their hearts content and every desire. He offered boundless knowledge to those who prayed and sought wisdom. He revealed the mysteries and secrets of the world to those in desperate search of spiritual truth and enlightenment. He provided clarity to those regarding the uncertainties and mysteries of the world. Mercy and salvation were granted to anyone willing to kneel and plea before his feet and seek repentance. God accepted prayers from those requesting absolution and atonement their sins and wrongdoings.

History would eventually come to prove many times over that the single act of returning Tree ultimately changed the trajectory and outcome of man's fate and their relationship with God. The king's popularity flourished and over time as he secured a large fan-base of gathers and followers. He would eventually establish his own gathering and legion of devoted worshipers committed to the sole purpose and defense of spiritual warfare. The spiritual battle waged over centuries between good and evil was now leveraged by the appointing of nobles and kings over man. The historical feud between two opposing forces was persistent and everlasting. However, God kept a personal scoreboard placing a single star across the sky like simple pins to account for his many triumphant victories.

6

The Reunion

Adam drew closer to Tree and Eve finding the pair still worn and consumed with sleep. The rejoicing moment evoked a sentimental tone from Adam seeing his dear friends safe and unharmed. These emotions produced within Adam feelings of joy and happiness as he exhaled a deep sigh of relief from his nostrils. His face carried a long-drawn-out smile that demonstrated that he was content with the prevailing outcome. Adam sat down patiently between Tree and Eve fully absorbed in the moment. He watched over the sleeping duo while relishing over the spoils and beauty that Eden had to offer. The wholesomeness and generosity of the gentle land was truly unmatched. Eden was primed real estate serving as an oasis for all the inhabitants and residents livening within the parameters of the walls. Adam thought of his family and fell into a melancholy state of silence. He swelled with shameful repugnance that his family could not share in the spoils of such a bountiful paradise. Adam thought about Cain who had never witnessed or experienced the splendors of rich and fertile grounds. But before Adam could sink further into his thoughts, he was distracted by the aching sounds of muffled moans which drew his attention. It was Eve holding onto her the small bulge protruding from her tummy.

Eve awoke to find Adam standing over her and was somewhat shocked by his sudden appearance. Joy and excitement surged through Eves body carefully raising herself from the ground to embrace Adam in her arms. "Awaken Tree!" Eve encouraged. She was enthralled with glee and excitement. Tree was still resting and was not yet ready to begin toying and playing around having grown exhausted of Eve's practical games. "Awaken Tree." Eve repeated. "Adam has returned." She celebrated loudly. Upon hearing Eve's announcement and mention of Adam's name Tree instantly awoke to find herself staring down at her dearest friend. It was moments such as this that Tree cursed and damned her rigid design. She wished for animation to possess joints in her arms which would allow for the flexibility of a warm embrace

"Thank you" Tree asserted impulsively. "For standing by me. You are truly a dear friend." Adam was touched by her words, "You are more than welcome." Adam replied. "You should think nothing of it." He humbly deflected, "I could not let you leave us, without telling us the story you had long before promised to share." Tree produced as solemn smile over her face that served as her response. She was moved by Adam's candor display of modesty and kind words. It was obvious to see that Adam loved her dearly and though unspoken he could not fathom the thought of her absence from his life. "Why yes, of course" Tree laughed out, "Indeed I promised you a story and so a story shall I deliver to you." Adam agreed with a nod and sat down on the grassy meadow beside Eve.

Seeing Adam sitting comfortably with his legs positioned and crossed in a childlike manner. The regressing image of Adam appearing eagerly patient to hear Tree tell a story was comical if not amusing to observe. Tree could not help but snicker at Adam as he attempted once again to mimic the pre-pubescent childhood pose. Adam was excited to have Tree share one of her fanciful tales. He turned his attention over to Eve with glowing excitement drawn over his face. "Are you ready?" Adam asked with growing eagerness. "Yes I am." Eve responded precariously. "I would love to hear a tale from Tree if nothing more." They propped their heads and dropped their shoulder waiting patiently for Tree to share her story.

"This is the story of Antelope, and Elephant," Tree began, but before she could start her tale Adam stopped her. "Tree, I have heard this story many times." Adam interrupted. "Please be kind and tell us a new and original tale; one that Eve and I have never heard before." Tree was shocked and somewhat impressed by Adam's recollection of her whimsical tales and stories. She was caught off guard by the spontaneous remark however was prepared to rise to the occasion. She paused for a moment to search the library of her mind the perfect story. Tree and Adam shared an extensive history between them dating back to childhood. Adam unlike Eve had already heard most of Tree's orations and tales.

Tree managed to recall a story she had never shared with Adam. At the time she believed that the fable was much too sophisticated for Adam's young mind to grasp and comprehend. But now he was mature and appropriately aged in size and wit. Adam was perfectly seasoned to retain the bulk and yolk of this imaginative tale. Without sparing another moment Tree began. "Have I ever told you the story of "Hyena and the Riverbed." Adam thought for a second and but could not recall having heard of such a story as Hyena and the Riverbed.

Adam shook his head, "No I do not remember ever hearing such a tale." Tree smiled triumphantly inviting Adam and Eve to draw closer in preparation to hear her tale. "Come closer my children and hear my story." Eve and Adam did as Tree instructed and perched themselves against the base of her broad body and trunk. They sat silently like children patiently waiting for Tree to begin her story.

"There once lived a Hyena who didn't know that he was a Hyena. All the other Hyenas said he was out of his wits because he did not behave and conduct himself like other Hyenas. This Hyena believed in his heart that he was a Lion and carried on behaving as such. Hyena went about the land wreaking havoc and causing mischief. He growled and would give chase after neighboring animals. His silly antics and mischievous deeds were often met with bursts of laughter amused by depth of own conjuring and ingenuity. The animals of the kingdom labeled Hyena delusional and out of his wits paying little mind to his pranks and antics. They began to accept Hyena's lunacy and would sometimes play along by fleeing and scattering frantically as though pretending to be frightened by his prowling presence. Hyena gave chase the animals chase however his flimsy legs, and small paws could hardly keep up let alone give him the strength needed to take them down. It became apparent that the poor creature Hyena was very much misguided and confused. On many days Hyena could be seen loitering amongst the pride of lions. He often hung around and hunted alongside the fierce pride. In his heart Hyena truly believed that he was a lion and would not be convinced otherwise.

One sweltering day when it was much too hot to hunt or graze. All the animals gathered around the riverbed attempting desperately to quench their thirst and sooth themselves from the scorching sun. Hyena who was now infamous for his strange behavior as a pretentious lion soon appeared. Hyena ignored the crooked looks and sharp glances he received from the crowd of onlookers. They whispered and gossiped among themselves mostly critical of the uninvited guest. Hyena appeared unbothered by their actions and drew little concern over the matter. He learned long ago to ignore the repulsed and guarded looks he received from crowds jaded crowd. In viewing himself as a lion, Hyena was unbothered by the looks of contempt and disdain received from the others. The tension and discomfort they felt only helped to reinforce the narrative and belief that he was indeed a lion and that they were all unnerved by his presence. Hyena trotted and pranced about in willful ignorance of the critical onlookers. He accepted their insolent glares and harsh looks as indication and confirmation that he was truly a fearsome and formattable predator.

The hot sun and dry weather drew Hyena to the riverbed upon which he discovered what appeared to be the entire jungle in attendance. The animals were lounging and relaxing in and around the riverbed. Hyena drew excitement at seeing the large gathering of animals and decided this was the perfect moment and opportunity to showcase his hunting skills. Hyena did not think twice or give much consideration to the mindless idea and thought of taking down prey. He began to prowl stealthily drawing himself lower to the ground to avoid detection. He was prepared and ready to pounce on and attack the next unsuspecting creature to cross his path. Unfortunately, for Hyena the next mammal to pass by him was lady Elephant on her way to the drink from the riverbed. Elephant saw Hyena perched on the floor and regarded the strange behavior as odd. Elephant exercised caution being aware of Hyenas senseless reputation. She deliberately made attempts to steer away from the mischievous creature. Hyena misinterpreted Elephant's attempt at evasion as clear sign of fear and trepidation.

Elephant like many of the others traveled to the riverbank in search of relief from the blazing sun. Hyena was socially inept lacking the basic cues of observation. He failed miserably to notice how irritable and annoyed Elephant appeared as she was not in a playful mood. The scorching sun managed to corral and bring together all different walks of life to the riverbed. Each creature seeking asylum and refuge from the heat. The riverbed had become a sanctuary for those looking to escape the unbearable elements. The public cooling area offered the inhabitants a place to cool off and quench their thirst. The air around the riverbed was peaceful and serene. Calmness fell over the gentle land and over the water. Suddenly without warning Hyena jumped out from the grassy fields lunging high into the air. However, Sadly, he miscalculated his attack and missed his mark and fell directly into the river. The loud crash startled Elephant and caused water to splash over her eyes and face. Elephant produced blaring outcry that sounded from her trunk. She reacted instinctively out of self-defense and used the base of her dense long nose like a giant club to connect violently against Hyenas body and torso. The blunt impact hurled the frail creature out of the water and into the air landing face first onto the ground.

Instantly the crowd of animals who had been watching and observed the entire ordeal roared out loudly breaking into a symphony of laughter. Elephant at seeing that it was the mad Hyena who had startled her became further annoyed and enraged, "What is wrong with you!" Elephant yelled, "Do you not understand that you are not a lion. Just look at your ears, your nose, and even your paws. You are fooling yourself pretending to be a lion." The crowd roared on louder. The heckling sounds of their taunting laughter began to upset and irritate Hyena. "Why are you doing this to yourself?" Elephant asked with flagrant ridicule masked beneath her breath. "I am so a lion!" Hyena shouted back, "I am as much a lion as you are an elephant." Just then Elephant blew from her nose heaping gust of water that drenched and soaked Hyena. "That should cool you down," Elephant scolded. "It is apparent that the hot sun has baked your mind." The crowd broke out into another uproar of laughter. The roaring sound of their cheers attracted the attention of more animals who began to gather around. They were curious to see and learn as to the source of amusement and commotion taking place. The wavering crowd were surprised to find what looked to be a soggy and frustrated Hyena in a contentious and heated argument against an obnoxious and oversized Elephant.

Hyena was aware of the sizable crowd gathering around him. He could hear the sound of their taunts echoing in the air. The crowd mocked and made fun of poor Hyena with ill intended remarks and false encouragement "Be careful Elephant!" Shouted a voice from the crowd. "Exercise caution when facing the self-proclaimed king of the jungle." The audience burst out into roaring laughter once again overcome with amusement. The crowds unsolicited remarks only help to further feed and fuel Hyena's already fiery ego. It was common knowledge in the kingdom that the lions were the most stubborn and prideful of Gods animals at the time.

Hyena looked around and spotted his would-be clan off in the distance. The pride of lions that Hyena often associated himself with were sitting sideline watching on in merriment and amusement. They entertained themselves at the expense and embarrassment of their friend and acquaintance. Hyena ran quickly to their side and began to relay to his friends the affront in which he had just experienced at the hands of Elephant. Hyena rattled on as though the pride had not been witnessed the incident as it just occurred. Hyena began to regain his confidence as he attempted to rally up his mates suggesting that they retaliate by ambushing and taking down Elephant. "It would be best if we acted now!" Hyena insisted. "Before Elephant attempts to retreat." However, no one was moved by Hyena's rallying call. "Come on now, let's get her." Hyena pleaded desperately to the others however not a single creature in the pride budged or stood up to answer or respond to Hyena's request and call. "I thought we lions stick together?" Hyena shouted in fierce and affirming tone. "I suggest that you watch mouth and mind your manners." Warned one of the elder lions growing rather impatient and annoyed by Hyena's audacious behavior. "As you can already see." Answered the fierce and rather intimidating lion looking back to look at his fellow pride. "Real lions do stick together. No of us have been fazed by the declaration of your mistreatment and abuse. As we see it, Elephant has not offended anyone in the lion pride or family." The onlookers fawned over the climatic action unfurling before their eyes. The audience waited to see the dramatic outcome and conclusion of the whole debacle. When nothing happened the tense and drawn-out crowd quickly offset the veil of silence with an eruption of incorrigible banter and laughter.

"You idiotic fool!" Elephant shouted harshly at Hyena before the raging crowd. "Those lions are not your kin and only use you to help gather food. Tell us, do you ever get to feast or enjoy the spoils of your collective labor? Or are you left to eat at the scraps of meat and bones that are leftover as indigestible remains." The flowing mixture of disrespect and humiliation had filled its brim and soon Hyena was foaming with anger and outrage. Hyena reacted impulsively to the offense suddenly lunged down off the cliff in an aerial attack after Elephant attempting to take down the large beast. Hyena found himself unmatched and his aerial assault foiled by Elephant who managed to grab hold of the feisty beast by the limbs. Elephant twirled Hyena over her head before releasing the helpless creature once again high into the air. This time Hyena would find himself landing in the shallow end of the r. The riverbed now served as the perfect arena and stage for and audience to watch on in entertainment and laughter as Hyena struggled to stay afloat.

Hyena who did not know how to swim flopped and splashed about wildly in desperation to reach dry land. No one attempted to jump in the water to save Hyena from his drenching fate. Instead, the antagonizing crowd watched on consumed with laughter and amusement at Hyena's mistreatment. He felt an indescribable sense of embarrassment and shame after witnessing his lion pride and family joining in on the fun. Hyena struggled to paddle and reach the other end of the river. He worked tirelessly to the point of exhaustion until finally he managed to crawl onto the shore. Hyena felt utterly defeated and susceptible to self-loathing and pity. He sulked with embarrassment feeling utterly defeated and humiliated.

It was then that Hyena spotted a reflection of himself through clear fresh water. Hyena found himself staring into the water unable to turn his gaze from the image looking back at him. It was as Hyena was seeing his image for the very first time. He appeared shocked and nearly bewildered by the discovery that he was indeed a hyena all along. As though having been stirred awake from an enchanting dream, Hyena was now confronted with the sobering reality of truth. He felt an overwhelming weight of shame for having denied his identity and neglected his lineage. The taunting sounds of ridicule and laughter traveled across the water. Hyena listened to the unsavory mobs hurling unflattering comments and insults at him. Hyena was annoyed and irritated by the demonstration of ill humor being had at his expense, He snapped suddenly and began to laugh hysterically along with crowd. The strange heckling sound of Hyenas laughter was unnerving and caused those laughing in the crowd uneasiness. Hyena appeared struck with hysteria and madness as he taunted menacingly.

He threatened vengeance on those who dared to mock and ridicule him. "Count your days!" Hyena threatened the jungle while scouring his gaze over Elephant ant the lion pride especially. Hyena retreated into the dark forest laughing hysterically. Hyena settled near the outskirts of the borderlands where no animals dared to travel and as result Hyena was never seen again." Tree ended her story.

The abrupt conclusion of her story stirred commotion and confusion amongst Adam and Eve. The questionable tale lacked the basic moral ingratiates needed to constitute for a well-balanced tale. Tree's bland story was remarked by Adam as lacking critical protein and fiber. "But whatever happened to Hyena?" Adam asked, "No one knows," Tree answered, "because no one cared enough to follow after him." "This was truly a strange tale," Adam joshed playfully. "It may truly be your worst story yet." "I think I understand," Eve answered seemingly enlightened by the wisdom of the tale. Stretching her hands outward to meet Adam's palms. "Listening to the story I could only think of one thing. That was where were Hyena's pride and family?" Eve questioned curiously. "Promise me Adam." Eve turned suddenly to face him. "That you will never allow any of your child to wander about aimless and confused like Hyena. Swear to me, that our children and descendants will know God, and will choose to serve him as their mighty creator."

Adam was confused as to the reasoning behind the warranted request. However, he willfully consented to Eve's request. He felt sentimentally provoked by Eve's belief and interpretation of the story. Adam was tired after hearing the long-drawn-out story and drew a long and exhausting yawn. The gesture was easily taken as an offense by his restful bystanders who took little consideration of Adam's exhausting journey to arrive at Eden. Eve was riddled with questions to whether the burden and weight of her interpretation had a depleting affect over Adam. Tree was left pondering whether the fable had caused Adam's to fall into a state of sleep and boredom. Neither Eve nor Tree's insecurities surfaced in Adam's mind as he sat comfortably at the base of Tree's trunk. Adam sat stoically relaxed in deep contemplation over the meaning and interpretation behind Trees story.

A smirk ran over Adam's face in recounting Eve's keen interpretation of Tree's tale. Adam nestled his hands together and placed them gently beneath his head. "Allow me a moment to rest and ponder over your thought." Adam turned over his body only to expose his backside. He scratched his rear and murmured indistinguishable words before falling fast asleep. Eve and Tree could only look on with bewildering astonishment and amusement. They found themselves consumed with delight and playful laughter at Adam's spiraling descent into exhaustion. The two declared that it was best to allow Adam time to rest peacefully. In the meantime, Eve agreed to prepare a meal for Adam after he awakens.

The pampered lifestyle and generosity that Adam received while in Eden became the customary treatment. Adam was praised and celebrated for his triumphant return to Eden as well as revered for his proficient mastery and knowledge of care taking. Blessed with multiple fortresses Adam was a man presently occupying two houses and homes. His only regret at the time was that he could not live or exist happily in both worlds. To be in two places at once was to Adam a godly feat that he believed would help to resolve to his current predicament and dilemma. His contemptuous struggle with duality and wanting to live and exist simultaneously in two places at once would become his unraveling and undoing. Adam felt challenged by the mortal limitations set over his very existence. This desire itself would become the foundational premise and predicament of man plight and descent. The burdening baton would be passed on by Adams descendants who would inherit the pursue and desire of conquest. Those of longing souls will eventually attempt to duplicate and replicate the omnipresent and celestial powers of their master and God. Adam was now inspired in his purpose and advocacy of spiritual equity and inclusion. He imagined his descendants having access to supernatural powers achieved through God like wisdom and knowledge. Adams defiant will and boundless curiosity would become man's defiant attribute and quality. Adam's descendants would carry on the will and dreams of their prophetic ancestor. Adam held the firm belief that man would one day ascertain the ability to mimic if not replicate the omnipotent powers of their master and God.

7

The Beckoning

The birth of Abel marked a celebratory and special occasion in Eden. God who was most excited at the thought of rejuvenation made a rare and unannounced visit to the garden appearing suddenly before Eve and her child. "You have done well." God commended Eve before severing her from the newborn. "Allow me a closer look." God insisted inspecting the infant creature thoroughly. The removal and examination of her newborn produced tense feelings of uneasiness. Eve had grown particularly fond of the new infant creature and was beginning to establish a nurturing bond with her newborn. God commanded that a large celebration be held to honor the arrival of their newly crowned prince. "Today we celebrate!" God announced, "The natural transition and passage of life into this world. This precious creature will reign over this kingdom until the time comes when I will call him to reign over the heavens." The proclamation held an all too familiar tone, his speech resembled that of a similar announcement made by Tree in her introduction of Adam. God was quite pleased with him-self, all his careful planning and tireless efforts had not been in vain. The birth of Abel proved to be a most triumphant day for the mighty king. Abel signified an opportunity at redemption for the king. His birth offered God a second chance for to fulfill and complete his masterful plan. God had managed to somehow overcome the obstacles and hurdles placed in his path to secure a worthy successor to inherit his heavenly throne.

The entire kingdom worked tirelessly in preparation for Abel's celebration. Abel being the rightful descendant of the king received royal treatment and benefits entitled to any child born of nobility and high rank. Abel's cradle was designed with the softest materials. His bedding and spread were fashioned entirely from the softest lamb's wool. The guards and railings of his crib were accented with rare and beautiful flowers namely roses, lilies and blooming orchids. The newborn prince was highly favored, and beloved by all the creatures in the Eden community. Eve in her association to Abel as his mother and matriarch received collateral praise. She had been elevated from her lowly station to assume the ranks of queen with regards to the noble prince.

Eve was revered and highly regarded throughout the kingdom for having giving birth to their messiah. She had endured the strenuous and exhausting task of childbearing. She completed the scared act and experience of bringing life into the world. The reward for her painful sacrifice was found in the tender eyes of her newborn child. The gift of serving as a godly instrument and vessel evoked a sense of elevation and prominence within her. Eve was now filled with pride and joy. She happily accepted her promotional benefits that came with being Abel's mother and rightful caretaker. The animals in the kingdom began treating Eve more formally holding her in high esteem in accordance with her nobility and royal stature. Eve's name quickly became renowned and celebrated as the mother of the soon to be king. The notoriety and fame Eve received only helped to reinforce the premise and belief that she was indeed a queen.

Abel and Eve were favored throughout the kingdom. Not a single creature could walk past the queen and prince without acknowledging their presence. Many times, the animals would form lines and gather in groves to greet Eve and offer praise and blessings to her and her new bundle of joy. The inhabitants of the garden often went out of their way to catch a glimpse of Eve and her newborn child. Familiar and unfamiliar faces would often stop Eve in passing to offer their respects and pay homage to the young prince.

Eve, and Abel grew to became beloved symbols of Eden. The garden came to adore Eve for the tenderness and affection she displayed over her offspring. These naturally redeeming qualities exhibited by Eve helped to remove the stain and blemish from her mortal image. Eve demonstrated unquestionable obedience to her king and followed her master's exact orders and demands with unquestionable loyalty and servitude. Eve had submitted her will before the king at her own expense and detriment. The supreme being ordered that Abel be reared spiritually pious and highly devoted to fulfilling the grand plan. Eve managed to secure favor from her noble king as well assistance the garden community. She received charitable offers for support rearing and with childcare if ever needs. Eve's loyalty and unshakable faith in her king did not go unrewarded. Her unwavering commitment to her lord and master assured that Eve and Abel would be blessed with prosperity and good fortune.

Tree on the other hand had been reassigned shortly after the birth of Abel. She was tasked with daily duties and responsibilities as Eve's midwife. Slowly overtime the need for Tree' s support and assistance began to gradually dwindle. Tree was being called upon less frequently over the passing seasons. Tree served as her king commanded and accepted her assigned role as entrusted advisor of the royal family. Her duties included watching over Eve and caring after the new child just as she had once done with Adam. Tree seemed unexcited drawing little enthusiasm at the thought of revising the earliest stages of child rearing. Tree reflected over past experiences recounting the many hardships faced with raising Adam. She commiserated privately in her mind never daring to refuse or speak out against the assignment.

Despite all her vulgar thoughts and private complaints Tree could not help but recall Adam's childish antics which also drew a smile over her face. She remembered the difficulty and challenges faced during her experience rearing and raising a child. This time however

Tree was hopeful that with Eve's support the challenges faced would prove less difficult this time around. Tree had been assigned the secondary role as Abel's godmother. The noble position was bestowed unto Tree by non-other than God himself. She was expected to serve as a supportive figure in Eve and Abel's life. Tree understood that her failure to provide safety and security to the royal family would prove to be consequential if not fatal. Tree set aside her reservations casting away any doubt or ambivalence surrounding her assignment. She begrudgingly accepted the plight of her circumstances with humility and grace. And despite her personal grievances and several impositions Tree took on the matron role without pride or prejudice.

Tree was secure in the knowledge and belief that over time their bond would grow. The role and obligation of primary caretaker was extremely taxing and depleting. Tree understood almost instinctively that Eve was a new mother, and this meant that most of the rearing and nurturing of Abel would ultimately fall on her shoulders. Tree knew that any discord or misgivings in the keeping of the royal family would cast a shadow of disappoint over her name. She did not wish to be questioned about her competency and usefulness. The liberal fun spirited persona which Tree adopted during Adam's rearing and childhood was discouraged and strongly frowned upon. She was now being encouraged to assume a more conservative demeanor and approach with regards to Abel. God sought to avoid any repeats or mistakes made in the past. The king was very much intentional in his commitment to correct his previous errors. This time God refused to allow any mishaps or disruptions to derail Abel from fulfilling his preordained destiny.

Abel had a very fortunate and fulfilling upbringing. Like any child of royal stature and lineage Abel grew up adorned in the spoils of prestige and privilege. He was educated by the best teachers in the garden and was introduced at an early age to a host of moral ideas and ideologies. The education that Abel received would help grow and mold the young scholar's mind. As a student Abel would often succumb to boredom and find himself being easily susceptible to distractions. His attention deficit and explosive energy made Abel's schooling increasingly more difficult and challenging for his instructors who demonstrated exceptional patience and restraint. The pupil Abel was afforded a wealth of knowledge by inter-disciplinarians who offered their insight, and wisdom on topics and subject such as riotousness and benevolence. Abel was assigned directorial courses specifically intended for future leaders, kings and rulers of empires. The caveat to Abel's expansive education was that he was not to be taught or educated on the exitance of evil. God believed that the introduction of evil as a subject would only stir Abel's growing curiosity on the matter. As a result of his deprivation Abel grew up blissfully ignorant to the knowledge and existence of evil. He was shielded from negativity and guarded from vulgar and insidious topics. It went without saying that a large portion of subject matter were omitted and prohibited from Abel's curriculum. The robust education Abel received was intended to exact dignity and pride surrounding his royal lineage. However, the royal class exposure would only help to elevate Abel's sense of self-worth and riotousness. The young prince would ultimately grow up to become a susceptible byproduct of his status and class. Abel's ordained destiny undoubtedly elevated him to the highest ranks of the royal monarchy. Unlike Adam who was guarded and kept in dark regarding his ordained destiny Abel was granted the full access and knowledge pertaining to the significance of his value in the fulfillment of God's plan. And upon being made of his vital importance Abel began to demonstrate rather undignified behaviors and haughty mannerisms.

Abel grew up sheltered within the safe and comfortable confines of the garden. The world he was accustomed to seeing was unlike the harsh despairing world outside of Eden. Abel had never endured any pain or experienced any sort of grief or suffering in his life and rightfully so as God would not allow for any harm to befall his coveted prize. Abel would never be able to understand or fully grasp the notion of misfortune and grief. Abel who unlike his half-brother Cain would never endure the blistering pain and discomfort of having bruised and battered feet. The sort of pain that ensued after treading mercilessly against the unfertile and hardened ground. Abel would never experience or come to know the uncomfortable betrayal of hunger coiling tightly at his inner organs. The harsh reality of the world outside of Eden was an unfathomable and foreign concept for Abel to fathom or conceive. The strange deprivation of negative emotions resulted in Abel having an unbalanced and unhealthy emotional diet that limited his range and development. He lacked the principals of empathy and compassion the core qualities needed to be a fair and just ruler. Abel's upbringing in the secured utopian environment left him little need to consider the wants and desires of others.

Emotional intelligence, and sensitivity training lessons went untaught despite their many benefits. They served little purpose in the grooming of the would-be king and soon to be ruler of heaven and earth. Pain and suffering were considered foreign and remote concepts within the paradise of Eden where joy and merriment thrived. The subject and topic or man's indignation was forbidden and unspoken and would be condemned as blasphemous within the boundaries of the garden. God revered suffering as a mortal sin that only helped to stifle man's potential by anchoring his progress and impeding his spiritual growth. He renounced and forbade the teaching of negative emotions around suffrage. God deliberately outlawed and removed any degradational teachings that would undermine or fill Abel's mind with conviction. Abel was without a doubt limited in his capacity of understanding. He could neither fathom nor articulate with language or words the morbid sensations of misfortune and disappointment. Abel lived a protected and very much sheltered life guarded against the scorns and pitfalls which comes along the way. He received the finest treatment of any nobility and was waited upon daily. Abel ate lavishly and was well kept. His diet consisted of the rarest and finest foods offered by the garden. Abel was regularly fanned and kept cool with giant feathers and long blades of elephant leaves. It went without saying that Abel lived rather comfortably in Eden surrounded by provisional abundance designed to protect against the hurdles and hardships of life.

Not a single creature dared to reproach the royal decree or demonstrate anything other than goodwill and hospitality to the royal family. And even under the most unpleasant of circumstances the unruly affronts of the young prince went unchallenged. The animals in the kingdom did not dare to patronize the young boy or impose corrective action to Abel's arrogant and disruptive behavior. They were fearful of upsetting Abel believing that they would be severely punished. There was a sense of duress over the hearts of the inhabitants who were mindful that someday Abel would someday ascend to power and govern as their sovereign ruler. The timid inhabitants never reported Abel's misconduct to his mother Eve and hesitated at time to disclose their observations with his guardian Tree. The citizens of Eden were inadvertently participating in Abel's maladaptive behavior by pacifying his irreputable conduct. They were unknowingly enabling him by not correcting his infractions and oversteps. Able grew up without limitations and as a recourse he was able to cross boundaries without receiving the slightest reprimand.

Tree tried desperately to instill manners into the young boy however Abel was rebellious and strong-willed refusing to listen or heed any of Tree's teachings. "It's one thing to be crowned a prince." Tree mentioned privately. "However, to act and behave as such while entirely void of honor and integrity was a travesty to behold." Watching Abel grow up and teeter past the brinks of pre-adolescence Tree soon began to discover through his actions, and attitude that Abel was nothing like his father. Abel seemed to lack within him a distinctive quality and trait observed in Adam. He reserved little if any humility, empathy, compassion or regard for the lives of others.

The thought of treating others kind seemed overrated and unappealing to Abel. He was often drawn to question the warrant of such righteous deeds. Abel grew up living a life of privilege filled with luxury and entitlement. It was becoming readily apparent to Tree and many others in the community that Abel's callous behavior stemmed from Gods revelation designating him as their future ruler. The inherent benefit of knowing one's destiny no matter how grand or minuscule their plight was no longer regarded favorably in the garden. If left unchecked Abel would only grow more arrogant and self-consumed on his path and journey to adulthood. Abel was no longer a child however his public display of buffoonery demonstrated that he was not yet an adult. Abel's behavior and blatant disregard for others gained him the label and reputation of discourteous and impolite. The creatures shared their personal experiences at having been affronted by Abel in some form or fashion.

Abel in his rebellious phase was in desperate need of structure and discipline. However, he received very little reprimand for his conduct and deplorable behavior. He like any child thrust into privilege and great fortune would become susceptible to corruption. Abel was not impervious to the lust and allure of power which often left him feeling morally bankrupt and emotionally destitute. He grew up arrogant and inconsiderate to the concerns and worries of others. Abel had inherited a god complex in belief that no other life was more important that of his own. And all though Abel's life was blessed and highly favored, he was quickly becoming widely detested and privately ill regarded by the inhabitants of Eden.

Adam stayed true to his custodial obligations and oath by spending his allotted time in Eden providing support with the rearing of his child. He kept his word and promise to uphold his commitment and responsibility to their son. Adam loved and cared dearly for his Abel and could often be found in the company of Eve and child. Adam spent a quantity of time rearing and raising his child as promised providing protection and mentorship to his Abel teaching him many unique skills and talents including the fine art of forging and crafting. Adam extended himself to assure that he was present on many joyous and celebratory occasions. Managing a private and secretive life was no easy feat to attempt let alone pursue. However, Adam was determined to keep his word becoming rather engrossed in his parental duties. He intended to honor and fulfill his solemn oath to God and never once attempted to shy away from the binding agreement. Adam was dutifully committed to accepting the wavering premise and outcome of his present circumstances. It seems pertinent in describing to the reader the very burden and weight of Adam's present dilemma. He often dwelled privately contemplating over the inequities of his contractual arrangement.

Adam's primary focus when visiting Eden was geared towards spending time with his child. He displayed tender love and affection for Abel that demonstrated his devotion as a father. The extent of Adam's guardianship was confined, and limited. Despite having free range in the garden his interaction with his son felt somewhat restricted and supervised. Adam was limited to teaching life lessons that aligned with the king's purpose and overall mission statement. Adam was not permitted the liberty of teaching Abel candidly. He was denied the necessary freedom to exercise comprehensive support for his child. Unlike the rearing of his first born, Adam was unable to teach or prescribe lessons and life curriculums deemed valuable and necessary for a growing boy brimming the cusp of adulthood.

Adam was discouraged from teaching Abel useful life skills like engineering snares and forging tools. No tools or weapons of any sorts were prohibited to formed in Eden. As was the act of slaughtering and killing of any creature or animal residing on the sacred grounds. The limitation of Adams supportive role as father often conflicted with his intention and pursuit to exercise full parental control over his son. To Abel the provisional title of father, and provider were conditional labels in which his mother was happy to fulfill. Eve spoke highly of Adam during times of peace and neutrality and dishonored his in moments of anguish and contention. The term father became an eerie connotation that seem to dissipate and evaporate over time. The implicit title began to serve as a term of inclusion and less synonymous with the explicit role of provider-ship. Adam did not bother to teach Abel how to scavenge or search for food. As a native of Eden Abel would never need to hunt or search very far for sustenance.

Adam was but one man occupying two worlds: two homes, and two separate identities. It went without saying that man's greatest endeavor and feat was attempting to exist and occupy multiple spaces at once. His narrow-minded ideals of managing a dual lifestyle were founded firmly in unrealistic goals. Adam was able negotiate his custodial presence requesting amnesty for time off to spend with his family. God was partial to Adam's appeal and offered clemency to his request. Adam was given free range to choose from any of the seven days created by God. Adam arranged to spend three of the seven days inside of the Eden with Eve, and his son. God declared that Adam was to share his time evenly allocating his presence and energy between families. He was given the liberty and freedom to choose from any three days of the week he wished to occupy the garden and was encouraged to stay longer if he chose fit. On the Sabbath Adam was given the freedom and will to choose whichever house or home he wished to reside. Sunday was granted to Adam to choose of his own desire and accord his preferred place of residence. Adam often wished that he could mesh the two families together to make them a solid unit. However, Adam knew that the king would never allow him to incorporate such an idea.

The concealment of a second family was no easy task for Adam to accomplish, however he managed to elude his family for several decades while maintaining the peace and sanctity of his home. Adam understood that to sustain and fulfill his obligation and promise to God, he would need to be concoct a clever if not pious excuse. Adam needed a plausible reason that would grant him clemency from his home at least three nights a week as needed to uphold his promise.

Adam fabricated a story for his family detailing the source of his turmoil and inner troubles. He declared with growing urgency the dire need to offer penance and seek forgiveness from his father. His deplorable admission was followed by a performance of uncontrollable sobs and tears. Adam proposed the idea for a three-day pilgrimage of which he vowed to fast and pray, tirelessly for God's mercy and forgiveness. Strangely Adam's mate did not attempt to challenge or discourage him from the path and direction of his pursuits. His mate was obliged and receptive to Adam's request especially after observing the depth of his turmoil and troubles. Adams partner acknowledged that Adam needed support and agreed that seeking out his father's pardon and forgives would help to ease the tension and trouble which seem to plague his heart and mind.

His mate did not discourage or dare to sanction Adams decision to seek out penance by way of pilgrimage. Adams partner accepted his reasoning without the warrant or need for further questioning. In the eyes of his mate, Adam resembled a wrongful child seeking to make amends for having wronged his father. Adam shared with Cain the source of his condemning troubles however failed to disclose the weight of his infractions. Adam explained to his son in somewhat of a codded language that a single act of disobedience could be considered hubris. The damnable act of not honoring thy father can change one's fortune and fate; possibly hurling them into the depths of grief and misfortune. This was Adams redeeming attempt to instill the values of grace and forgiveness into his son's heart. "It is important to honor thy parents, but morse so thy father." Adam explained. "For a fathers vison for his creation and child will often exceed the boundaries of his own limitations." Adam began to sob woefully before his son. "It is my hope that you one day forgive me for the chaotic conditions in which you were placed." "But I do forgive you father." Cain pleaded emotionally. "I know that none of this your fault. Please do not leave us father." Adam silenced Cain's anxiety and worries by placing a finger over his son's lips. "Do not worry son, for I would never forsake or abandon you." Adam reassured Cain. "Initially I was prepared to tread the ends of the world in search of absolution, and reconciliation.

However, in consideration to the needs of my family I have limited my altruistic pilgrimage to assure that that my voyages do not exceed the length of three days."

Adam did as he had promised often returning from his pilgrimage to the warm reception of his family. His mate and son rejoiced regularly in celebration of Adam's safe and triumphant return. Cain who was most affected by his father absence would often run to greet and embrace his father. Adam's home was simple and modest filled with unconditional love and happiness. It was easy to understand why Adam chose to commit and allot Sundays to staying at home with his partner and son.

Adam's favor and priority to his original family did not go unnoticed by the sentinel of prying eyes. Initially Adam's visits to Eden went undeterred as he would spend a vast amount of time with Abel in the company and watchful eye of Tree. To retain his fidelity and honor to his mate Adam began to deliberately ignore Eve. He often removed himself from her presence and treated her cordially as though nothing between them outside of Abel existed. In a sense of the word Adam began to demonstrate and display less affection for the queen shortly after the birth of the prince. Adam's visits to the garden began to include less interaction with Eve and was more focused on Abel, and Tree. The triangulation of affection shared between Adam, Abel, and Tree was somewhat exclusive. The pyramid of love offered no radius or circumference in which Eve could be pegged. It was not Adams intent to behave maliciously towards Eve or beseech her with cruel or unkind words. Adam's only fault at the time was that he did little to offer Eve an explanation for his crass and crude behavior. Internally Adam harbored the fear of getting too close and succumbing to the seductive prowess of Eve's allure. He was taunted by this notion of her enchantment and set out to avoid Eve as much as possible. In their seldom encounters and interactions Adam held conversations with Eve however he kept the dialogue short and brief. He managed to subdue the untamed and the raw emotions he felt for Eve like the leashing of a wild out of control hound. Adam was unwilling to cross nor breach the boundaries of intimacy and affection with Eve. He appeared somewhat afflicted and slightly unresolved at having been played and pawned as a tool.

Adam would often deny Eve's romantic advances at courtship. He simply refused to allow to be fooled and baited a second time by her seduction. Adam resolved the matter by confessing his love and affection openly that he was satisfied and happily in love with his mate. The declaration created a great deal of contention and hostility between Eve with Adam. The humbling rejection of Adam's interest was deeply upsetting and unsettling for Eve to accept. She began to experience the strong negative feelings which she could scarcely describe. She was embittered with a host of emotional turmoil including jealousy and resentment. The conflicting feelings that served as primal emotions were now being viewed as secondary needs. The loss and absence of Adam's intimacy and interest seem to devastate Eve. She felt as though she somehow being punishing by Adam for her part, and role in his domestication.

Over time Eve began to display feelings of restlessness and agitation over the present circumstances. The livid emotions which she harbored began to manifest and form into feelings of anguish and resentment towards Adam. She detested the fact that Adam was choosing to prioritize his family and home over herself and Abel. Adam's visits to the garden were beginning to serve as a mocking reminder that she could never have him for herself. These intense and truly frustrating emotions began to weigh over Eve causing her grief and great distress. She began to demonstrate her discontent and frustration with Adam by openly voicing her grievances. Eve shared her candid displeasure surrounding the permit of Adam's absence and unreasonable allowances from the garden. The propaganda of Eve's petition and complaints helped to reveal the tension of her mounting insecurities.

At the height of her desperation Eve attempted to exercise her influence and rank over Tree. She demanded that Tree implore Adam to stay in Eden and neglect his other life and family. However, each time Eve made this demand, she received neither cooperation nor compliance on Tree's part. Tree's refusal to aid Eve in her mission and ploy to secure full custody of Adam only help to further the struggling and strained relationship. Eve harbored a deep sense of resentment in her dutiful role sensing a gnawing and uncomfortable feeling brewing within in her. A mournful sense of sorrow began to manifest in Eve causing her deep sadness. It was the dawning realization that she had no autonomy or will over her life.

Carrying years of frustration and bitterness began to have a negative effect and toll over Eve. She was no longer the bounty of beauty that Eden had once propositioned and fallen madly in love with. Eve had let herself go in the sense of the word presenting as lofty and unkempt with a lace of thinning hair covering her head. The once healthy and able-bodied Eve was now feeble and shrilled exposing somewhat of a skeletal frame. Eve seldom smiled and preferred to be away in isolation often keeping her distance during Adam's visit. Her odd behavior began to garner attention from her son Abel who began to question the well being and sanity of his mother's. Abel was not entirely oblivious to the changes taking place in his mother's psyche. He took notice of her odd behavior and one day voiced his concern to his mother inquiring as to whether she was well. "Are you alright mother?" Abel asked with grave concern for his mother.

The question seemed simple enough having been based on Abel's observation of his mother declining health. Any other time Eve would have pacified her sons concern with an automated passive response. However, this time it seemed the symptoms of loneliness and depression had spilled over into her heart corrupting her sound sense of judgment. Eve looked over at her son who was standing tall and lean scaling past her in height. She felt as though the moment had finally arrived declaring in her mind that Abel was old enough to hear the truth. It was at this moment that Eve would make the dire if not miscalculated judgment of unloading and unpacking the source of her sorrows and trouble onto her son.

"I am sorry son." Eve cried out, "But I can no longer bear the pain in my heart." Eve began sobbing uncontrollably. Seeing his mother in distress caused Abel great grief and sorrow at having to endure the weight of his mother's wallowing tears. "Why are you crying mother? Abel asked drawing grave concern to his mother's troubles, "Tell me what is troubling you?" He plead to his mother to explain the reasoning for her condition and current affliction. Eve inhaled deeply and exhaled a heavy sigh of exhaustion. Eve slowly regained her composure and looking into the face of her worried son she began to divulge the sources of her trouble and inner turmoil. Through Eve's disclosure Abel he would come to uncover the reason behind his mother's bitter feelings and growing resentment towards his father. Abel listened to his mother share her sorrows all the while trying desperately to hold back his own tears. Adam's implication as the source of his mother's troubles did not sit well in the chest and heart of young Abel. The soiling discovery of his father exploits seemed to plague and dampen his very mood and spirit. Abel found himself wrestling internally with his emotions after being bombarded with a somewhat bias version of the truth. He eventually came to learn of his father's betrayal to his mother by way of withholding the rare mineral of love and affection from her. Adams indecisiveness and refusal to set boundaries seemed to be the running motif and theme in which Eve based her grievances.

Despite hearing his mother's complaints of mistreatment Abel was conditioned to pardon his father's neglectful behavior as inconsequential and meaningless. Abel lacked the empathetic lenses needed to understand or fully grasp the concept of pain and betrayal. Having been born of royal stature rank Abel was naturally preconditioned to receiving endless affection and praises from the inhabitants of the garden. Abel found it difficult if not impossible to process the unfamiliar feelings of heartache of un-requitedness. Despite having several exceptional qualities Abel was emotionally bankrupt and withdrawn. He was unable comprehend or navigate the transactional reasoning or value behind interpersonal relationships.

It was not until Eve chose to reveal the solemn and unspoken truth of Adam's secret life and family outside the wall that seemed to draw Abel's attention. Abel was skeptical at first but as he listened on his temper began to boil over with anger and outrage. Abel learned of the sacred oath and pacts which were settled and made on his behalf. He appeared upset by the contractual arrangements made without his consent or knowledge. Abel felt conflicted and somewhat confused by the ordeal began to foster feelings of resentment. He experienced a high degree of unfamiliar feelings and emotions he had never felt before. Abel began to draw assumptions behind the motive of his father's affection. He questioned whether the love he received from his father was natural and purely of his own free will and not ordained or forced on him by a higher power. Abel felt stoically awestruck and detached in state of disillusion and loss for words. He was unprepared to face the shattering truth of his father's infidelity and betrayal. Abel felt as though he had been deceived and misled regarding the falsehood of his upbringing. On this day of reckoning Abel would uncover the devastating truth about Adam. The scandalous discovery would send his hero spiraling into an abyss of nothingness. The respect and admiration that Abel held for his father began to slowly diminish and disappear before his very eyes. Abel was now angry and upset by his father betrayal. The massive structure of Adam which Able erected in his mind to honor his father was now under demolition. The eroding statue and monument of Adam was being chiseled and torn down to reflect his present state of anguish.

Abel was unable to fully process the host of strange and unfamiliar emotions swirling inside. He found himself growing hostile and tempered by the allegations made against his father. Abel became overwhelmingly flustered with emotion and declined Eves attempt to sooth and calm him. He refused to be pacified or coddled like a child by the arms of his mother and caretaker. Confronted with shame and embarrassment Abel reacted like any young adult would. He resorted to crying out in anguish before scurrying off and running away. Able was hurt and desperately sought relief from his troubles. He was seen running towards forest in the direction of Tree. He raced eagerly to confront the matriarch and historian to confirm whether his mother's salacious story was true. Eve attempted to deter Abel from departing however, her efforts were pointless as she was unable to redirect or control her torn and anguished son.

Abel fled quickly running frantically through the garden in search of Tree. He arrived finally exhausted and breathless consumed with sweltering fury and rage. "What is the matter?" Tree asked voicing her concern. "What seems to be bothering you, Abel?" Tree asked again attempting to quell his fiery temper which at present time seemed more intense and fiercer than usual. Abel shared the news disclosing the source of his pain and anguish. The confused look of desperation poured openly from his eyes as he recited over his discovery. Abel needed to know whether his mother accusations held any grain of truth to them. He inquired as to the truth pertaining to the secret life of his father. Tree was shocked and conflicted somewhat emotionally torn by the sudden ambush of Abel's request. Tree felt compromised by her dutiful commitment to address Abel needs and relieve him pain and distress. Tree hesitated somewhat struggling internally on whether she should confirm or deny Eve's allegations. Tree justified her choice knowing very well that she had no right to refuse or deny the demands posed by the impatient and tormented prince.

"It was all before your time my child." Tree confessed openly attempting to quell Abel's temper. "You should not concern yourself or become distracted by matters contrived before your time." Tree quickly caught the course of her words and firmly tightened her lips embarrassed by her own mishap and blunder. Abel was not amused reflecting a silent and hostile glare. His cold and silent stare made Tree feel tense and uneasy becoming noticeably distressed by the intensity of his reproach in demanding an explanation. Tree did not attempt to further her objections but instead displayed compliance by drawing a deep breath of air and releasing a gust of air. The heavy sigh validated her feelings of exhaustion and defeat.

Tree did as Abel requested exercising unyielding obedience to the commands of her future king and master. She disclosed accurately all the answers to his many questions and inquiries. Abel demanded to know the purpose and reasoning for his fathers' extended absences and frequent disappearances. Abel secretly hoped for an alternative narrative and outcome different from his mother. However, he was instantly plagued with embarrassment as Tree would go on to confirm a similar narrative and tale shared by his mother just moments earlier. Tree explained the context in which she was familiar with Adam's other family and apologized for withholding the truth from him. Tree offered to share her personal experiences and encounters with Adam's other family. She hoped that her stories would somehow evoke compassion and empathy from the young man. Tree's intention to neutralize the anguish and rage that Abel was currently harboring. However, her plans failed terribly with Abel responding begrudgingly to the sympathetic request. Abel was now filled with contempt and outrage towards, Adam, Eve, and Tree. He demonstrated his disappointment openly by fleeing Trees presence to privately navigate the complexities of his emotions.

8

The Betrayal

Abel became consumed with the thought of his deception. He no longer enjoyed the company if his father's presence. He chose instead to remain at his mother's side during Adam's encounters and visits. Adam could not understand the reason or cause for the sudden change in Abel behavior and searched for understanding by posing his observations to Tree. Despite his many inquisitions Adam received no clarity over the matter. Tree was sworn to oath and secrecy by the young prince not to divulge any information to Adam regarding his discovery. These were truly tough times for Adam in his attempts co-parent and meet his role and obligations. He had no idea the feelings and thoughts that festered in the mind of his avoidant son. Abel no longer rejoiced over his father's scheduled returns. Adam began to carry the same weight of emotional baggage over his shoulder as Abel's embittered and resentful mother.

One day shortly after Adam's departure from Eden Abel approached his mother with a divisive plan that would permanently keep Adam bound to Eden. The appealing thought and notion of Adam's tenor and residency intrigued Eve who drew discretionary interest in Abel's plan while retaining an air of dignity and concern. The moment of reservation was short lived as Eve was left to navigate the roller coaster of emotions spiraling around in her mind. Fueled by unbridled passion and mischief Eve and Abel began to sort through the many discrepancies in their elaborate scheme. They shared and explored different scenarios until finally they concluded with what they believed to be a masterful and cunning plot. The plan was so vile and insidious that it seemed almost ironic that such a mischievous thought could be conceived in such a sacred and peaceful place.

Their sinister scheme was simple yet diabolical prioritizing function over form, however it was effective none the less. They conspired to commit the terrible act of killing Adam's mate and making it seem as though Cain had committed the terrible deed. Such an act of betrayal would devastate Adam deterring him from wanting to return to his home. "He will finally be ours." Eve celebrated pensively. "Your father will have no reason to leave or venture outside of Eden."

"Yes," Abel added growing giddy with eagerness and excitement. "Experiencing such betrayal would help to promote me as his beloved and favorite child. No longer will my father be distracted or forced to compromise or divide the bulk of his affection and attention."

Together mother and son conspired to conceive a deviant plan that involved the removal and assassination of a prominent figure. It was established that the perpetual framework of their plan needed to be disguised as an unquestionable act of foul play. This elaborately crafted ploy devised between mother and child seemed infallible and well secured. Abel was charged with excitement and peeked with intense eagerness and enthusiasm. He shared the details of his barbaric intentions with remedial intricacy and simplicity. It became obvious and apparent that Abel was unprepared and even worse unskilled to carry out the act of murder. Eve listened disagreeably to Abel unfurl his plan to use his bare hands to squeeze away the breath and life of his father captive. "And if I should encounter my half-brother Cain in my path, I will surely strangle him as well." Abel was youthfully arrogant and somewhat overly confident in his strength and abilities. He spoke belligerently with intensity giving little thought to the consequences of his action. Abel was dangerously possessed by the spirt of anguish and rage to the point of sounding violent and homicidal. Eagerness and anticipation seemed engulf and fill Abel's awry heart and nerves. Luckily it was Eve, his mother who managed to settle the anxiety and growing tension building in her child.

"I am impressed by the practicality of your plan." Eve complimented Abel, "However, allow me to offer a few suggestions to your cunning plan. These minor modifications will help to end our troubles once and for all." Leaning closer to her son, Eve began to whisper softly into Abel's ear to unfurl a complex and elaborate gambit. A delightfully cynical smirk began to cast over Abel's face as he listened to his mother's insidiously cunning and masterful plan. Abel appeared immature however his body and frame was sturdy peeking the cusp of adulthood. He intended to honor his mother by restoring the joy and bliss that was wrongfully taken from her. In the heat of the present moment of swelling rage Abel was willing remove and tear down anything or anyone standing in the way of his mother happiness.

"A very long time ago before you were conceived." Eve began to reveal. "Your father gifted me a small tool which I believe will serve us sparingly. She unveiled a beautiful small dagger; sharp and oblique carved entirely from ivory edged from stone. "Your father presented me with this gift during our courtship as a token of his affection." Her voice began to grow soft and dim, "He told me that he crafted the tool especially for me so as to avoid pricking myself when collecting flowers from the rose bushes." Eve began to blush uncontrollably recounting her many trysts and fun encounters with Adam. "And though I seldom found little use for the novelty itself. I kept it as a tokened prize demonstrating the gesture of your father's endearment and heartfelt love for me." The useful tool was designed to cut away and remove stems and weeds from the botanicals. The small dagger that Adam gifted Eve was intended as a useful tool for the green thumbed gardener, however, this was not the case. Eve showcased the dagger and discussed her plan to repurpose Adam's gift with the perverse intention of using the floral tool as a weapon. The sharply edged blade that was commonly used to slash and cut away flower stems was being grossly mishandled. The very gift that unified Adam's love for Eve would serve as the fatal instrument that would sever and tear apart the very fabric of his life.

Abel listened to his mother as she unveiled her sinister plot, he could not help but look on with glowing pride and admiration at witnessing first-hand the intricate craft of his mother's wit and cunningness. Naturally Eve illustrated every detail of her plan with uncontrived ease and precise clarity. The elaborate plot seemed almost unimaginative and tactfully preconceived as if stewing for some time in the back of the queen's mind. The fatal end of Adams mate had always been a dormant desire that Eve secretly longed for. Although Eve had never confessed it openly it was apparent that she was consumed by morbid feelings of jealousy and resentment towards Adam' partner.

"You will wield this tool," Eve announced turning over the dagger somewhat reluctantly to her unseasoned son. "Upon my instructions you will set forth and locate your fathers dwelling and home. Pursuit with caution." Eve warned. "Assure that you are stealthy as to avoid being seen observed." Abel was growing more anxious and nervous as he listened carefully to the set of directions being delivered to him. He paid close attention listening rather attentively somewhat anxious and nervous fearful of missing a vital step or some important piece of information. "...In entering the home there, you will find the wretched wench who holds your father captive." Eve placed her hands firmly over her son shoulders. "Listen carefully Eve urged her son. "When in the creature's presence you should muster all of your strength to successfully thrust the dagger into the being repeatedly in order to bring the creatures life to an end." Eve removed the knife from Abel's grip to effectively demonstrate the gruesome gesture. The exhibition of jabs and stabs sent a jolt of panic and fear through Abel's body, and very soon he found him-self trembling nervously confronted once again by emotions and feelings he could neither express nor describe.

Abel was grossly inexperienced and unskilled in disarming and taking down creatures. He had never slew or slain anything or anyone in his life. Abel had little desire to slaughter any of the subordinate creatures or animals living in garden. Heinous and sinful acts such as killing, and murder were banned and forbidden in Eden. Abel's heart pounded as his mind raced around the fatal idea of taking away another creature's life. The dreadful thought paralyzed him with overwhelming fear. Abel found himself growing rather nauseas and queasy with the unsettling thought. He did the best he could to hold back the thick wad lodged in the back of his throat. Suddenly without warning Abel began hurling uncontrollably spewing from his gut. Abel was filled with overwhelming anxiety and nervousness after realizing the bulk of his duties. It was clear by his reaction that he was unable to stomach the morbid thought.

"Mother, are we certain about this?" Abel was beginning to reconsider his commitment and involvement in the dreadful act. "Do not worry my son." Eve reassured Abel attempting to alleviate his growing concerns. "Rest reassured that the act of murder is forbidden within the realms of Eden, but do not forget my child that your journey will draw you far beyond the boundaries of our region." She pacified Abel with a comforting smile and a reassuring embrace. She held him tenderly in her arms which helped to restore his confidence and faith. A heavy sigh of relief escaped Abel's mouth after accepting the will of his mother. Abel was his mother's only son and like any child his age he valued the weight of his mother love above all others. It seemed that Abel was now being burdened with the task of fulfilling two dutiful assignments. He now assumed himself to be the protector of his mother's virtue and honor all while preparing to fulfill his purpose his destiny as ruler. Abel in his noble piety did not want to disobey any of the sacred laws of the land. His worse fear at the time was repeating the errs of his father and ultimately falling short of God's eternal love and grace.

"Mother?" Abel began to ponder and question. "What if I am unable to bring down creature?" Abel wrestled with a host of variable possibilities and outcomes. He riddled his mind with endless scenarios filled with barriers, and unforeseen hurdles. "What if the creature confronts me and I find myself unable to perform my duties..." Before Abel could finish, his mother silenced his worries by gently placing a finger over his lips, "My dear son," Eve said, looking deep into the elusive and wandering eyes of her young son. "You are a man now." She reminded Abel. "You are the most intelligent and most powerful creature to walk the face of this earth. You are wiser than a parliament of owls, braver than a pride of lions. You possess the swiftness and agility of cheetahs and leopards in their prime. Your resilience in the face of adversity remains unparalleled. This is why you have been chosen and selected deemed worthy to fulfill God masterful plan."

A moment of silence fell between the two as Abel was unsure how to respond. "You are destined for greatness," Eve added. "However, you must first learn to cast shame and doubt from your mind and heart fort fear is the cancer that lingers within. Do not be deceived by your own senses or question your capabilities. Instead walk in faith and stand tall with conviction that you are coveted by the grace of God." Abel was floored by his mother's heartfelt decrees. "Abel" Eve called to him suddenly. "In order to achieve greatness, you must first be willing to overcome all obstacles and challenge anything or anyone standing in your way." Abel was astonished and mesmerized by the powerful incantation of his mother's words which by the reception of his bewildering smile had fulfilled its intended purpose. Abel's confidence seemed to be fully restored to the latter stages of anticipation and excitement. Eve's short speech had captivated and enthralled the young man. Abel now overly inflated with an armored sense of self-assurance. Abel was like a naive child captivated by his mother's endearing words of affirmation and vote of confidence. He willfully accepted his mother's circumstantial doctrine as irrefutable truths.

"I will make sure to never forget your words when I become ruler" Abel assured his mother, "I am now ready to go forth and complete the task. Together we shall free father from the binds of his wretched confinement. "Eve listened rather supportive and stoked by her Abel's bolstering words and display of growing confidence. "No longer will father be forced to endure a mundane and meaningless life." Eve gleamed with joy and happiness, listening to her son profess his loyalty and commitment to their cause. Eve was confident and felt safely secured in her impenetrable belief that her plot would truly bring Adam home to Eden and restore happiness back to their lives.

9

The Treachery

The diabolical plot did not go as expected due to unforeseen circumstances. Adam did not return to Eden as expected. His unexcused absence would ultimately delay Abel and Eve's plan. It was not customary and very much unlike Adam to lose track his usual routine and schedule. However, after much delay, and prolonging the perfect opportunity finally arrived. The dastardly duo would finally get their change and opportunity to unfurl their devious scheme.

It was a cloudy misty morning when Adam arrived in Eden. A layer of fog covered the land smothering it in thick white smoke. The surrounding mist made Adam's pilgrimage to the garden a rather a difficult and challenging journey. He was somewhat looking forward to spending the next three days in the land of paradise. The peace and hospitality he received during his lodging and stay in Eden could hardly be considered a punitive sentencing. Eden was quickly becoming a haven and sanctuary for Adam. The luxuries of the garden offered amenities as well opportunity to unwind and decompress from the toils and troubles of his personal and private life. The call for rest seemed justified the last few days were filled with exhausting strenuous tasks. Adam had spent much of his time in the company his family carrying out much needed home improvements and attending to domestic affairs. The sum of his labor left his body sore and aching all over. These events helped to explain the reasoning behind his delinquency and unexcused absence. Adam was usually reluctant when the

106

time came to leave his family and home. However, this time he looked forward to relaxing his sore body and bones beneath the shaded leaves of Tree's and branches accompanied by his son.

In the thick of the mist Abel proceeded as instructed by his mother making his way in the direction and location of the grand wall. He made sure to keep near the rear edge and southern base of the wall as instructed by his mother. Abel would soon discover the unguarded exit and doorway leading out of Eden. Everything was going just as Eve had described it to him. Abel was instructed to seek out a place to hide and wait for his father's arrival before attempting to venture forth. Abel arrived as instructed however before he could cloak himself or find a suitable place to hide Adam appeared suddenly walking through the corridor of the unbarred gates. Abel panicked and was instantly engulfed with fear at the thought of being discovered and confronted by his father. Naturally Abel was overcome with the instinct sense to flee and run. However, the crippling fear he exhibited kept him leashed down like a hound removing any opportunity or chance to scurry away. Abel was subdued in a frozen and silent state of fear and panic finding himself separated only few short meters in distance from his father.

The mystifying cloud provided a thick veil white fog over the garden making it difficult for Adam to see clearly. He began to question the strange climate which impaired vision making the terrain more challenging to navigate. "What is going on here out here?" Adam questioned to himself out loud, "This is ridicules. I am unable to see beyond my own nose!" He was highly critical of the cloudy weather. Abel managed to quietly disguise himself in the background. He knelt before the encroaching sounds of footsteps. Abel's heart pounded uncontrollably thumping loudly from beneath his chest. He heaved in a gust of air holding it in the upper cavity his chest. Abel braced himself for impact and closed his eyes to for the unavoidable collision. He felt the caress of brisk of air whisking past his face as Adam crossed his path. Abel slowly unclenched his jaw and released his nerves drawing out a heaving sigh of relief. He looked up and searched around but lost sight of his father amidst the dense fog. With very little time to tarry or waste Abel made his way past the gate darting through the stoned corridor and out into the desolate world.

Abel took off running, moving stealthy through the elongated corridor in quick and swift manner. He emerged on the other side in full view of the barren wasteland. Abel immediately hastened his stride stopping for a moment to take in the less than illustrious view. Able seem uneasy and somewhat disappointed by the desolate wasteland outside Eden. "How does father manage to live here?" Abel questioned. "In this abysmal wasteland of emptiness." Abel for the first time was witnessing the harsh reality of the outside world. "The land here is hardened and unfertile without flowers or trees." Looking around and finding only the scattering of rocks, and large stones placed casually around the landscape. The strange fog and mist began to lift and clear up slowly subsiding beneath the rays of the bright sun peaking over the mountaintops. Despite the grotesque landscape and poor infrastructure, the addition of sunlight seemed improve the aperture and overall look of the mundane landscape.

For a moment Abel found himself drifting off plagued with natural curiosity and childish intrigue. He imagined himself being reared in such unforgiving world and immediately shuttered at the thought. Growing increasingly more aware of his intrusive thoughts Abel awoke instantly from the brief daydream shaking away any unnecessary thoughts and distractions. He recalled with outrage and bitterness the sole purpose of the mission. Able kept his eyes on the ground searching desperately for any signs and clues to direct his path. He recalled his mother's words and instructions encouraging him to venture towards the mountainside as told by Adam. However, Abel was viewing firsthand the monumental structures of cascading mountains that decorated the entire landscape of the foreign and usual world. Abel began to consider how premature and partially flawed their superficial planning now seemed.

Abel was resourceful and resiliently clever. He was determined to fulfill and complete dutiful task set before him. Being an attentive tracker Abel managed to uncover and follow a pair of footprints engraved in the dusty trail which he believed belong to his father. He followed the trail down a beaten and narrow path. Abel tracked the fleeting pattern of footprints disappearing slowly before him. Abel felt lost walking blindly without any sense of guide or direction. He considered the thought of returning home to the garden to accept the outcome of disappointment and ridicule from his mother. However, looking back at the vast distance and range of his progress he could scarcely view the grand wall off in the distance. Abel decided it best to continue the path of his journey under the pretense and guidance of blind faith. It wasn't much longer before Abel would arrive at the mountainside and base of his father's cave and dwelling.

Standing outside the cavern den peering nervously into the entrance Abel found himself gripped with fear. His nerves quaked uncontrollably trembling nervously at the entranceway of his father's home. His gazed deep into the dark dwelling finding the shadowy cavern engulfed in abysmal darkness. Abel was hesitant and growing more nervous and anxious with every passing moment. He contemplated the possible dangers that awaited him inside the dark cave. At the peak of his anxiety Abel felt consumed with an eerie sense of impending doom. Abel began to slowly draw his weapon from his side. But with unsteady and quivering hands he nervously fumbled the sharp dagger dropping it on the floor. Abel knelt to retrieve the dagger, and in keeping low to the ground he remained crouched at an angle.

He entered stealthily past the threshold of the doorway stepping beyond the precautionary boundaries of safety. The cave was pitch black as Abel struggled to maneuver quietly inside. His senses and eyes seemed to betray him as he struggled distinguish objects before him. Abel stepped forth cautiously furthering deeper into the cavern den with each silent step. He counted his every step with precise calculation measuring the exact distance between himself and the cavern doorway. In his mind Abel had already mapped out an escape route if the need called for him to retreat or flee. His clammy palms seeped with nervous moisture, and dew. Cold sweat began to form down Abel's face and neck until very soon it saturated his chest and back. Abel appeared uncertain of what to expect next but furthered into the cave blindly against his intuition and better judgement. In his mind he compared the murky darkness before him against the thick fog experienced earlier. Abel saw no difference between the spectrum of blinding extremes. He managed take a few more steps furthering into the mysterious cave where he could scarcely make out the tinted environment surrounding him.

Abel moved as quietly as possible, his feet treading lightly against the dirt. He struggled to tame his composure tempted by the urge to retreat but fought against the impulse of his quivering nerves. Abel misplaced his footing while stepping forth and landed on a brittle bone of some sort. The snapping sound echoed through the air and seized his body and nerves causing him to stiffen and tense up. In a heightened state of frozen vigilance, Abel waited patiently for any reactions or signs of movement.

Abel stood frozen and statuesque with his foot still planted firmly over the fragile bone. His chest pounded violently as his heart throbbed. It seemed that the bone was not the only thing broken at that present moment. Able struggled to retain his composure collecting what little that fortitude that remained from his broken and shattered confidence. The ricochet of echoing noise that caroled Abel's nerves eventually subsided and filled the quaint cavern with silence. Abel managed to settle his nerves and, in a sense, tuck his heart back into his chest. Suddenly he felt a hand grip hold of his shoulder from behind. Abel gave out a terror-stricken shriek, and turning his body he reacted instinctively by striking the creature with a hard blow causing the shadowy figure to stumble and fall to the ground.

Abel did not wait and capitalized on the momentum by hurling himself onto the ground in search of his assailant. On the dusty floor the two bodies wrestled, tussling and tumbling in a relentless and heated struggle. Abel using ample force and strength was able to over-power and pin the creature down long enough to secure his weapon. Once in hand Abel drew forth his dagger holding the sharp object into the air. Abel did not hesitate or stop for a moment to consider the value and worth of the creature beneath his blade. He plunged the dagger into the creature's body piercing deep into his victim's chest. Abel stabbed repeatedly until the wounded the creature fell into a limp and lifeless state.

The injured creature attempted to scream and yell out from agony and pain but found it impossible to muster the strength to call out for help. The sharp tool managed to puncture the creature's neck. Abel could feel the dwindling strength of creature beneath his weight des-perately gasping for air. He trembled frantically from the jolting shock of nervousness surging through his body. Abel was overcome with instant remorse for his grief-stricken actions. Abel appeared perpet-ually mortified by the unforgivable sin he had just committed. A sud-den rush of fear and paranoia took hold of Abel as he began to panic. The creature lay lifeless on the ground with a warm liquid seeping out from the wounded openings. "Finally, it is done." Abel declared giving an exhausted sigh of relief. He had completed the sinful objective as-signed to him by his mother. Abel was now burdened with the daunt-ing task of strategically placing the weapon for discovery. He intended to incriminate Adam for the heinous assault being that he would not return home for three days.

Abel would learn that even the most elaborate schemes and plans are subject to mishaps and unforeseeable flaws. In the throughs of darkness Abel could not clearly make out the face of his victim. He searched madly through the dark cavern to locate the dagger but was unable to find the murder weapon. On his knees Abel searched the ground combing the dusty floor for the misplaced dagger. His hands trembled nervously as he searched the ground for the lost tool. His fingers accidentally stumbled over the fallen creatures' cold dead feet.

Abel nerves instantly unraveled as he abandoned any hope of finding the lost dagger. He rose quickly to his feet and dashed clumsily towards the brightly lit exit and doorway. Abel darted out the the cave consumed with fear and terror. The frightening feelings began to subside only after he had placed enough distance his spaced between himself and his victim. Abel made stride in his path and was now heading in the direction of grand wall. He began to feel safe after gaining traction and furthering his range. Strangely a bizarre transformation began to place over Abel. The emotional dilemma that he struggled to manage began to perverse into feelings of excitement, and delight. "I killed something or someone in that cavern." Adam dwelled for a moment over the conflicting thought and realization of his actions. He realized suddenly that he was unable to positively identify or confirm the creature that he had slaughtered. This gnawing enigma only seemed to hinder and impede his excitement. Abel entertained the thought of returning to the cave to confirm his kill but dismissed the senseless idea out of fear of being discovered and exposed. Abel returned home triumphant with the high hopes of having fulfilled and completed the task by slaying the right creature. Abel single handily removed the largest barrier and obstacle in the way of his family's ascension and succession. The triumphant victory of Abel and Cain was won through deplorable and disgraceful means.

The very creature that enchanted his father and anguished his mother was now removed. These thoughts and more surfaced through Abel's mind as he scurried back towards the grand walls leading back into Eden. He ran toward the gated entrance way moving quickly through the stony corridor. Abel breached Eden's wall and quickly steady his stride to a calm pace and stroll. Abel was overcome with a rewarding sense of calmness and reassurance after returning home to the sanctuary of Eden. Abel returned to Eden with a newly discovered appreciation for the fertile beautiful garden and landscape. He rejoiced over the notion of sanctuary believing Eden to be a haven free of foreign and domestic dangers.

Abel's boisterous ego and flaring pride gave him little time to notice or gaze down at his feet. For had he taken the time to look down and examine his body he would have taken account to the trail of blood visibly smeared beneath his heels. The pitter-patter of blood trailed lightly over the blades of soft grass. A dreadful act had been committed on this day. The first symbolic stone had been hurled. It served as the premise of feuds and battles between good and evil. A declaration of war had been affirmed through the immoral and tactful act. The loss of an innocent life would lead many to famously speculate on the exact events that occurred on this faithful day. It is unknown as to why God chose to stand aside and remain idol to the unfurling events without offering reproach. No-one knows or understand why the king did not intervene an interject to stop Abel and Eve from executing their plan. However, it appeared that God was turning a blind eye to the unjust acts of his creations. The king would assume a plausible degree of deniability and responsibility over the spiritual warfare that would be waged on earth between forces of good and evil.

10

The Undertaking

Cain arrived home in a joyful mood. He was delighted for having secured diner so early in the day. He walked into his home and was instantly mortified at discovering the butchered body of beloved mother lying lifeless on the ground. Cain ran to his mother's side and cradled the creatures slain body in his arms. He began to weep and sulk uncontrollably while holding the lifeless body of his mother in his arms. Cain imagined that a wild ravenous beast had straggled into their lair and savagely attacked and killed his mother. Cain could still feel the warm liquids of his mother's spewing down his chest and legs. "Mother's blood is still warm." Cain detected. "The predator may still be nearby." He rose quickly to his feet with fiery ember burning deep in his eyes.

Cain burst through the cavern doorway searching madly about for a clue of some sorts. He spotted a strange set of footprints that resembled his own. The smeared and bloody prints were plastered against the barren and dusty floor. Cain followed the trail of blotched footprints trailing over the ground. The scorching sun and sweltering heat help to dry the rosy stains of blood directly into the beaten path. Cain was in active pursuit of the crimson trail which would lead him to the grand wall. It was there that Cain would discover the doorway and entrance into Eden. Cain was bewildered by the monumental structure. He hesitated for a moment before choosing to enter. He passed through the corridor to discover a foreign and unfamiliar world. The land around him was marvelously draped by pastures of plush greenery. Cain was astonished to find himself surrounded by a vast amount of unfamiliar and foreign creatures flourishing abundantly around him. The creatures and inhabitant of Eden strolled idly by Cain with some stopping to observe the strange newcomer. Cain reflected similar sentiments towards the strange onlookers. He reflected the strange gawks and stares he received with identical sentiments of confusion, and disbelief.

Cain ignored the strange glares received from the unsightly onlookers. He paid little attention to the odd reception he received from the curious inhabitants. Cain did not lose his focus and moved quickly through the land following the faint trail of blood. He managed to keep track of the fading imprints trailing into the wild and eerie area of the forest. Cain navigated through untamed jungle and emerged to find an enormous Tree placed at the center of the forest. Cain took special notice of the thick wild vines that draped down the large tree like coiled ropes braided and twined loosely. The garden of Eden was a strange and unfamiliar for place for Cain to absorb. Cain appeared rather uneasy exploring the botanical setting viewing the wild vines that cascaded and hung down from the ginormous tree. His senses seemed to intensify in full view and presence of the enchanting tree. The veil of organic vines swaying back and forth resembled that of a majestic serpents luring over unsuspecting prey.

Cain was helpless to the intricacies of his imagination. He was becoming frightfully weary of the of the new territory and environment. The rural setting of Eden was fertile and soft nothing like the landscape and environment which he had become accustomed. Cain was understandably uneasy traveling through the murky jungle. He moved cautiously through the unfamiliar forest navigating the strange and foreign landscape. Cain was growing more anxious with every step his body filled with trepidation and fear. He was eager if not determined to escape the botanical labyrinth and as a result he began to sprint. Cain lengthened his stride running nervously through the estranged jungle fearful of the unknown. His mind conjured up a host of dangerous outcomes and possibilities hoping to avoid being blind sighted or ambushed by the hostile and dangerous assailant. Cain remained vigilant preoccupied with the thought of coming face to face with murderer of his mother. In his imagination the encounter would prove to be fatally unpleasant for the disheartened perpetrator.

Cain ran through the uncharted garden without an outlined or clear destination. He was unsure as to where his feet would take him but believed that each step was bringing him closer to uncovering the attacker. Cain had lost track of the stained footprints however was determined to search every crevice and corner of the garden until he discovered the creature whose steps and footprints resembled his own. Cain paced on in search of an outlet and escape from the botanical forest but luckily managed to secure a path leading toward an opening. He was drawn to the narrow exit and stepped out to find himself surrounded in a paradise of beauty and splendor. He walked about in astonishment having never seen such a vast assortment of beautiful flowers perfectly arranged and spread openly among a fields like natural decor. The visual of the land was extravagantly spectacular and decadently arranged. Unbeknownst to Cain he was entering the very heart of Eden.

Cain furthered his journey and stopped momentarily to rest and catch his breath. He perched himself beneath a precariously large Tree. Looking around, Cain set his eyes on some delectable fruits that were placed randomly on the floor. Peering closer at the tasty morsels he began to recall a hint of familiarity with seeing the colorful fruits. A small fruit suddenly fell to the ground beside him. The sudden impact caused Cain to draw his attention up at the giant tree. Cain discovered exotic fruits hanging from limbs and branches of the fruitful tree. He was filled with a sense of estranged familiarity standing beneath the boughs of the massive tree. Cain examined the frame and body of the tree standing before him through nostalgic lenses. He felt as though he had seen this very tree before but was unable to recall the exact memory.

"Where have I seen this particular tree before" Cain began pondering to himself. He reached out and gently placed his palm on the tree. He felt the rigid texture of the tree drawing his fingers over the creases and crevices. Cain felt over wrinkles etched deep into the bark and skin of the familial tree. He struggled to recall lost and forgotten memories from his childhood and youth. Cain questioned the source of illusions that replayed in his mind. He began to recall an instance during his youth when he had been introduced to a talking tree by his father. Cain looked questionably at the scaling tree standing before him with reservation and uncertainty. He was filled with ambivalence whether this was indeed the tree that spoke to him when he was a child. This persistent line of questioning caused Cain to further investigate his suspicions and uncover the truth. Placing the side of his face against the bulky tree Cain could feel the sensation of warmness radiating beneath the layer of hardened skin. Listening closely Cain could hear a pattern of thumping sounds resembling a heartbeat. This confirmed his suspicion that this was indeed the tree that he encountered long ago as a child.

Responding to Cain's warm caress the stoic tree began to stir and awaken from her deep slumber. Tree looked down and believed herself still half asleep and dreaming. She gazed down in astonishment at being met by a strange and unfamiliar and visitor. Tree could hardly contain her surprise and excitement believing herself to be still asleep and dreaming. It was perplexing to conceive the strikingly familiar face resembling that of an identical yet youthful version of Adam standing before her. Cain favored his father sharing strikingly similar traits and attributes in his posture and demeanor. Cain was the splitting image of his father in his primed age. Tree was led adrift by the youthful being standing before her. However, upon hearing the stranger speak her delusions instantly vanished confronted by the familial voice.

"You are Tree." Cain firmly declared. "You know my father. "Tree was shocked and outright surprised to find Cain of all people standing in Eden. Her eyes widened, "But how did you get here?" Tree asked somewhat startled and confused seeming rather tense and uneasy by Cain's presence in the garden." "I am searching for an invader." Cain answered pensively somewhat annoyed by Tree's lack of hospitality. "I do not understand how you arrived here at the garden, but you must leave this place now." Tree warned, "It is not safe for you here please go." She urged his departure, but Cain rejected her counsel with bold disdain and crudeness in his tone. "No. I will not leave," Cain declined boldly. "Not until I find the murderer of my mother." "Wait!" Tree interrupted. "What did you say?" She asked in utter disbelief. "My mother is dead!" "Cain repeated with overwhelming anguish and pain lodged in his throat. "But how can this be?" Tree responded appearing confused and somewhat troubled by the unfortunate news. Cain retold the events leading to the gruesome and rather disturbing discovery of his mother's slain body.

Tree could no longer bear the intense story and was nearly brought to nauseum over the horrific details. "I have tracked the creature into these parts." Cain continued. "I believe that the killer resides here." Cain concluded the emotional events leading to his sudden appearance. Tree attempted to draw forth in her mind a cast of plausible suspects that could have committed such a heinous act. "My God!' Tree cried out, "I hope what I am hearing is not true. "God!" Cain repeated. He began to grow hostile and more intense with the mentioning of the king's name. "What do you mean God?" Tree was becoming rather unsettled by Cain uncivil and aggressive demeanor. "Who is God?" He demanded to know. "Is God the one responsible for my mother's death?" Cain lashed out demanding that Tree provide a deposition to his inquiries." "That is not what I meant" Tree attempted to deescalate the tense situation after observing Cains growing temper. "Tell me then, what do you truly mean by God?" Cain demanded an answer and scoured menacingly at Tree with a fierce and maniacal gaze. The unpleasant interaction quickly morphed into a moment of interrogation between the two. Tree felt herself growing more uncomfortable beneath the prowling gaze of her disgruntled visitor. "I have a nagging suspicion." Cain remarked aggressively. "That you know a lot more than you are leading me to believe." "Tell me now!" Cain demanded in a vengeful tone. "Who was it that slaughtered my mother!"

Tree was a bit shaken and taken aback by Cain's intensity. Seeing his facial expressions, she recognized that he was in no toying mood. She began to fear the unimaginable intentions of her tormented intruder. Tree was unsure what to expect from Cain's impulsivity. "I am not sure." Tree responded nervously. "I do not know who has taken life, but rest assured I will notify your father immediately regarding this matter." "My father?" Cain repeated questionably, but why would my father be here."

Feeling rather uneasy around the seemingly distraught and tempered Cain, Tree felt the possible need and warrant for an intervention. "Permit mmm, mmm, me a moment to send for mmm, mmm, Macaw." Tree nervously stammered over her words. "Our resident messenger bird will fetch your father to us." But before Tree could make the call she was distracted by a strange noise. The sound of shuffling plants postponed her outreach. "Wait," Cain whispered listening attentively to the sounds of laughter drawing near. Cain could hardly believe what he saw before him. It was the sight of his father walking arm to arm with another mate. Cain was bewildered and confused by the sudden and unexpected appearance of his father He did not know how to react. Adam reacted with similar sentiments of shock and disbelief to find himself standing face to face with his first-born son.

"What is this?" Cain audaciously questioned his father with a tone of disgust and disbelief. "What are you doing here father, and who is this creature in your company?" Cain directed his questions and demands to his father while fixing his gaze over Adam's shoulder at the enchanting creature standing in the background. Her beauty and poise seemed remarkably familiar. "Who is this creature." Cain demanded to know growing increasingly more impatient. "And why does this creature look so much like mother?" Just then, following shortly behind his parents, stepping out from the bushes entered Abel. He was surprised and shocked to find Cain inside Eden and immediately viewed him as a threatening invader in their home. Abel upon witnessing his brother for the first time was feeling rather intimidated. Cain stood proportionally large in stature and firmer in tone. Abel felt outranked in comparison to his own lean and fragile frame. "And who is this?" Cain fired away appearing irritated and annoyed with exhausting task of uncovering another unfamiliar face. The moment of silence drew an air of awkwardness over the perplexed group They glanced back and forth each shooting nervous and uncomfortable looks at one another.

Adam stepped forth to bring an end to the discomfort of swelling tension building around them. "How did you arrive here?" Adam smiled rejoicingly with open arms to offer his son a warm embrace. Adam was genuinely happy to see Cain inside of Eden. His appearance at the garden confirmed that his family were no longer barred or excluded from entering the realms of paradise. Adam attempted to accredit the good fortune of Cain's sanctioning to his sacrificial pilgrimage. "It seems God has forgiven us of our sins." Adam praised happily. "And is allowing us free range and access into to his sacred land." Cain listened to his father's daunting and futile attempt to provide an appeal. Looking beyond Adams embrace over shoulder Cain was distracted by the two strangers standing idle in background resembling mother and child. Cain quickly deduced the familial dynamics observing the creatures shared common attributes and smiler traits. Cain seemed particularly interested and fixated on the creature Abel cowering closely behind his mother. Cain studied over the young creature taking special notice to the blotches of redness stained beneath the young man's feet. The sight of blood instantly hurled

Cain into a state of blind rage. He pushed Adam aside and set forth to confront the unlikeliest of suspects.

"You!" Cain shouted angerly. He directed his fury and anguish towards Abel who at the time was quaking uncontrollably behind Eve. "It was you who slew my mother!" Adam was thrown and confused by the strange declaration, "Slew your mother?" He repeated but received no answer from the afflicted son. Cain launched after Abel like a madman pulling from his side a long hunting blade. The sharply forged tool resembled the very dagger used to slay his mother. Cain's dagger was much larger and specifically designed for the formidable and skilled hunter. Cain descended over the Abel pummeling the boy and his mother to the floor. He was fueled with fury and blinded by rage. Cain was prepared to end the boy's life and slaughter his mother as well if given half the chance.

Adam responded quickly by inserting himself between his feuding sons. He managed to pull Cain off his brother however the interference only helped fuel the flames of Cain's fiery temper. He lunged after his father and tackled Adam onto the ground. Adam, and Cain tumbled and tussled wrestling like ferocious beasts rolling around on the ground. The two heavyweights pummeled and pounded at one another with each contender demonstrating a unique exhibition of grappling techniques and moves. The two opponents appeared evenly matched in strength and fortitude as they exchanged contentious hits and hard blows. Abel observed the heated battle in utter terror and quickly took refuge behind his mother. It was safe to assume that Abel was afraid outright frightened of enduring the wrath and vengeance of Cain. "What have we done." Abel cried out cowering behind his mother. Eve did not have an answer and responded with arrogant silence. Her arrested attention was engrossed in the gruesome brawl taking place in front of them.

The dagger switched hands numerous times going from Adam to Cain's then back again. The garden would set the stage for an unprecedented and monumental fight taking place. The dispute between

Adam and Cain centered around virility and vitality. The cycle of natural energy undoubtedly favored the incorrigible youth as Adam would painfully come to learn. In watching the two fighters battle it became triumphantly clear that Cain was much faster than his fierce, yet sluggish opponent. It was without a doubt that the Cain would seize victory by overtaking his father. Cain reserved unimaginable strength as he lifted his father off his feet before slamming him hard onto the ground. Adam attempted to raise himself off the floor but found it impossible to move or sit up let alone raise up his head.

Cain stood over the body of his battered father. "This is why you urged me to avoid and this region and area." He looked up at the Eve and Abel and grew angry and tense. "You lied to mother and me about your secret pilgrimage and path to penance." Cain was infuriated by his father's poor deceptive conduct. "For decades you willfully pursued this spiritual voyage that removed you from our home." Cain stood over Adam with a glaring look of disappointment at his father's dishonorable behavior. "You chose to spend your days here surrounded in a paradise of bountiful beauty and splendor." Cain was clearly nursing feeling of anguish and resentment towards his father. "You deceived us!" Cain poured out openly "You left mother and I within the harsh ruins of unfavorable conditions. You abandoned us father and for what; an enchantress with whom you bore a demon child."

Adam struggled to lift his head up to face his son. He listened with muffled clarity the embittered frustrations and convictions of his anguished son. It was as that moment that Adam began to realize how his decision affected his family. The impact of his prolonged absence from his house and home caused severe symptoms of longing and loneliness to form. There was a distinguishable void that filled and consumed their home in times of his absence. "Was mother not enough for you?" Cain chastised his father with contempt and disrespect etched in his tone. "Had you loved, and cared for mother and me as much as you care for these creatures..." "Stop it!" Adam interjected, "Stop this madness." He urged Cain to end his aggression. "That is not true, I love your mother..." "No!" Cain remarked. "I will not stop until you understand that you are a man and not a God. You were never made to occupy multiple spaces or call more than one kingdom your home. Despite your lofty goals and incredible ambitions, you cannot exist in two places at one time."

A menacing look cradled over Cain's face somewhat diabolical and disturbing. He turned his attention over to his brother and began to address his frightened sibling, "You have taken someone very precious from me younger brother, however I will correct this err by making us both motherless orphans." Cain made the bold declaration wearing a sinister grin over his face. He shifted his gaze to Eve who appeared equally stricken with terror if not more fearful than Abel. "Your son has unjustly murdered and removed my dear and beloved mother. I would be remiss to not return the endearing favor."

Wielding his dagger with expert skill and precision Cain coiled the weapon over his shoulder and hurled the dagger forth sending the deadly instrument into the air. He aimed the dagger directly at Eve with the intent of striking down and killing the creature. The fatal impact would ultimately settle the vengeful score by bringing an end to Eve. Adam's lowly angle allowed him full view of unfortunate outcome. He was unable to muster the energy needed to raise himself from the ground to intervene. The entire scene panned out gradually with the set of events playing out slowly in his mind. Adam watched the flying dagger cutting slowly through the air. The sharp dagger gradually neared its mark with only inches away.

Just then, Abel pushed his mother out of the way leaving himself exposed, and vulnerable to the fatal blow. The dagger instantly pierced in the chest dropping him instantly onto the ground. Abel fell helplessly on the floor a few feet away from his mother. "Nooo!" Eve cried out hysterically. She balled and wailed loudly calling out to her befallen son. This was truly a sad and dreary moment for Adam after having learned of the loss of his beloved partner just moment earlier. He would now have to grieve two lives after witnessing the death and slaughter of his youngest son. Abel laid on the ground with his eye open gazing at his father as he gasped desperately for air. Adam stretched his arm outward reaching out to Abel. He attempted with to crawl over to his son, but sadly his body would not budge or move.

Adam pleaded for his son's life calling out to his fallen son. "Please get up son, rise my son." Despite his encouragement Abel was unresponsive to his call. Watery tears filled Adam's face as he shut his eyes tightly in hopes of awakening from this nightmare. Adam was in denial and refused to accept the series of fatal events that just took place. He clasped his palms tightly over his face until his nose and brows began to ache. Adam prayed that this was all a nightmare and that he still fast asleep. However, as he slowly pried his hands from his face Adam was disappointed to discover that he was not dreaming. This was no hallucination or delusion his senses had not failed him. Adam was looking directly at the cold dead body of his son, nestled in the arms of his mother.

Grief stricken and childless Eve poured away sobbing desperately over the body of dead child. Seeing Abel on the ground lifeless seemed surreal to Eve. She offered a deafening outcry which was immutably pitched and prolonged. Her lips shaped the intense sounds that carried the bulk of her emotions. Eve appeared afflicted and painfully scorned from the bowels and pits of her mournful soul. Cain was unfamiliar with Abel and could never have predicted that his brother would commit such a noble act. The honorable gesture conflicted with Cain's internal perception of his brother causing discord and dissonance. He struggled to maintain the image and view of Abel as a heartless monstrous beast. "I do not understand what is going on here," Cain stood pondering mysteriously to himself. "What kind of monster sacrifices their own life to protect their mother from harm or danger?" Abel actions and sacrifice made it observably clear that he was no monster. There was no explanation as to why Abel sought the need to protect his mother from the path and trajectory of impeding danger. "Do you see it now father?" Cain laughed tormentedly. "What you have done." He attempted to absolve himself of any wrongdoing or responsibility in having committed the fatal offense. "Some creatures will kill for the mother's honor and affection. Just as there are those who will lay down their very lives for the same noble cause."

Adam with relentless effort managed to crawl over and be near his befallen son. Upon feeling the Abel's cold lifeless body Adam began to sob and weep uncontrollably. Cain was disappointed by the current outcome of his present circumstance. He was growing impatiently intolerable to the presence of his father. "How does it feel father." Cain declared with disdain and temperament in his voice. "To have two lives weighing over your soul." Sadly, this would be the last time that Cain would ever join his father in Eden. His last image of the land was that of Adam and Eve huddled over the lifeless body of Abel covered in blood and drenching tears.

Cain prepared to take his leave overcome with the intuition and sense to excuse himself from the dreary situation. "Where are you going?" Adam demanded to know but discovered he was unable to restrain or hold Cain back. "Where are you going?" Adam demanded once again. "Home!" Cain yelled back just before disappearing into the jungle following the path from where he arrived. "Please, tread slowly!" Adam pleaded loudly to the empty space before him. An unintelligible response and noise came from deep within the jungle, however Adam was unable to clearly hear or decipher the distant and final words of his son.

Eve was weeping uncontrollably holding onto the body of her deceased son, Adam did what he could to console her but was helpless in his crusade to aid in her grief. His thoughts and attention were fixed on the fresh tender face of their befallen son. His empty eyes lay open fixed upward as though staring far and beyond the skies above. Adam and Eve had done all that they could for their son. The last thing left was to shut Abel's eyes closing them as if granting him permission to rest and sleep forever.

Adam and Eve sat together quietly grieving over the tragic loss of their beloved son. The hurt and pain made it difficult for either of them to look up or face each other. They kept a private vigil with their eyes fixed over the body of the deceased son. The moment of silence spanned for some time with each choosing in their own special way to mourn and honor the memory of their lost child. "I should go." Adam announced painfully, "I need to make my peace before Cain settles his mother's body into the earth." Please do not go." Eve pleaded whole halfheartedly "Do not leave us here."

Eve began to weep and cry out inconsolably. She begged Adam to stay but he did not respond. Adam carefully raised himself onto his feet despite his body still feeling tender and sore. The sound of Eve's weeping and sobbing outcries poured louder and more intense with each breath and cycle. She was tormented and consumed with anguish and outrage while at the same time plagued with guilt, shame and regret. Adam pivoted slowly to make his way out of the garden to find his son. Adam did not intend to appear insensitive to Eve's outcry however he was also grappling internal with conflicts surrounding grief and loss. It was decided however it went unspoken that both creatures required some distance and time apart to bereave and mourn their loss(es).

Eve cries carried a deep and sorrowful longing. Her loud bellowing weeps resonated profound misery and pain. The sounds of her painstaking cries were heard echoing woefully throughout the entire garden of Eden. The startling pitch of her woeful screams alarmed and disturbed the quiet serenity of the otherwise peaceful land. Eve's mournful outcries caused neighboring animals to scurry and retreat from the vicinity. Just as well flocks of nearby birds began to flee from their homes and branches desperate to escape the tormenting sounds of Eve wallowing in agony.

11

The Collusion

Tree performed the sacred prayer calling out to the king. "God." She whispered, "I fear that a great travesty has unfolded in your paradise. Abel has been slain by Cain, meanwhile Adam has fled from Eden. Eve is ridden with grief and has fallen into a devastating depression the likes of which I have never seen or witnessed." Tree found her self-alone endorsing her grievances out into the open air. She reported all that had taken place reciting with vivid clarity the precipitating events that led to their undoing. Tree paused briefly staring off at the distant moon. She found herself staring up at the twinkling stars her eyes fixed on the glowing moon. It was with heavy heart and deep sadness that Tree began to accept the overwhelming disposition of her present circumstances. She was bothered by fact that God was listening to her cries, and that her master did not appear to sooth her grieving soul.

"God!" Tree summoned her king once more this time with a flaring impudence in her tone. Tree's act of hubris and harsh approach seemed to provoke the intended response as sudden chill pierced through air, "Do not raise your voice to me!" God warned speaking to Tree in a condescending and condemning tone, "Just because you cannot see me, do not assume that I am not present." Tree was overcome with panic startled by her king's impromptu appearance. "My apologies your highness please forgive me." Tree pleaded in sorrowful attempt to reconcile for her misdeed and crass behavior.

"You are sadly mistaken." God reproached Tree. "If you believe that your eyes can surpasses that length and range of my vision." Tree did not attempt to look up or respond to the king's rhetoric. "My plans have once again crumbled falling into the ruins by the misconduct and disobedience of man." "But why not consider Adam." Tree cried out. " Choose him with to reign in heaven with..."

"No!" God answered quickly disqualifying Tree's recommendation. "Adam has become tainted and soiled through his alliance and allegiance. It appears that even his son has become corrupt. Did you not witness this for yourself in plain sight?" God's arrogance and insensitivity pained Tree dearly his patronizing words breached her tough exterior like a parasite gnawing away at her confidence. "Adam's spirit is tainted." The king explained. "His loyalty to the covenant has been deemed questionable. Adam will spend much of his time on sabbatical squandering much of his energy and time in search for his mate's slayer. At the peak of denial Adam will dispute what he already knew to be truth. Sadly, when he finds no slayer and receives no justice, He will eventually return to confront inevitable truth. The startling revelation of Eve's involvement in Abel's demise would only help to further Adam's undoing."

Tree listened silently to the prophecies and predictions being cast down on Adam. Her mind worked quickly to decipher and comprehend her king words. Tree was bothered by the image and thought of Adam wasting his life and time on a quest-less odyssey. "Stop him!" Tree demanded forgetting her place once again. "Please, awaken Abel from his eternal slumber, before..." "I have already explained to you that I cannot intervene." God declared. "Not until I am summoned or called upon. Only Adam can bring back Abel and restore the life of his son."

The thought of resurrection excited Tree, "This is great news your highness." She pled for her king to share his knowledge. God looked at Tree as if annoyed by her ridiculous request but nonetheless he decided to offer her a clearer understanding. "Adam must repeat the sacred act and ritual in order to resurrect his son back into this world." Tree looked confused at her king as though not fully comprehending the extent of his explanation. An exhausting sigh came from the king, "Adam and Eve must reproduce in order to have their child returned to them." God shook his head in disappointment annoyed at the outcome of another failed attempt to fulfill his plans. "If only my stubborn begotten son would call out to me in prayer..." "But why would he?" Tree interrupted with callous disregard in her tone. "Why would Adam call out to you when your absence helps to conjure feelings of contempt and resentment within him." Trees emotional outburst surprised God and somewhat intrigued the king enough to hear out the full discourse of her proposal.

"I wish that you had you shown some interest in Adam and conducted regular outreach to speak with him routinely. As his creator you could have easily validated his existence by consoling his fears and concerns. But instead, you choose to confess and share your fears to me as your trusted confidante. I apologize my lordship if you have not noticed it by now, however I am a Tree. I am nothing more than a stationary prop forced to absorb the subjugated complaints and grievances of others." Tree was observably upset and filled with brooding anger which she displaced and directed towards her king. "You never once sought my consul or inquired upon my expertise regarding Adam before enacting your will. Had you chosen to involve me in prevalent matters surrounding Adam's disposition and development than some tragedies could have been prevented."

"Tread carefully." God warned. "For it appears you have forgotten your place." Tree was confronted by her king's growing temper. However, she refused to shy away from the subject and matter at hand. "With all due respect your highness." Tree answered sparingly, "I am a tree. I know very well my place. Being grounded is not a new experience for me." God was taken aback somewhat confused by the tense disdain and change in Tree's attitude. "You placed Adam into my custody assigning me as his guardian and caretaker. I did not ask for this role. But since then, I have grown to love and adore Adam to the point that I would choose his presence and company over yours." Tree's present conduct and behavior was unforgiving. Her sharp words cut deep into the heart and marrow of her beloved king. Tree wielded her words like a bladed dagger aimed to pierce and deflate the massive ego of the king. She appeared frustrated if not disgruntled to say the least. Tree was tired of being silenced and controlled by way of subjugation and fear. She decided that she would liberate herself from the shackles of her spiritual oppressor. Tree began to unravel rather quickly stripping away the fears and doubts which kept her powerless. She began to reexamine the passive practice of her silent obedience thru the lenses of bitterness and disdain. Tree was slowly beginning to accept accountability for her complicit silence. She began to recount and recall several failed opportunities to speak out and condemn her king's actions but instead she fearfully refrained. Tree reflected with anguish and began to feel infuriated and upset by her cowardly conduct and behavior. She reacted impulsively with an eruption of insults and unsavory words. Tree unveiled the contents of her heart by disclosing feelings which had been festering deep in her soul. She revealed a host of unsolicited and unwarranted emotions however this time she did not hold back. Tree was deliberate in her declaration. She had no intentions of retracting or reconciling her words with an apology.

God could sense the growing tension and hostility dwelling within Tree. He recognized with vague familiarity the contentious words that spewed from the mouth of his radical subject. Somewhat annoyed by Tree's display and conduct God was generously slow in his temperament. He demonstrated his futile amusement by allowing Tree the stage and space needed to further compromise and incriminate herself. "You are God!" Tree stated bluntly. "But you are also a creator and a father. Go to your son and relieve him of this anguish. Do not let your relationship with Adam fester like an untreated wound to grow diseased and eventually infect its host. Instead offer him grace and forgiveness for his mishaps and missteps and the many mistakes of his past and those which he has yet to commit. I pray that you do not abandon your son in his time of need. Your absence would only further to server the already strained relationship. It is ultimately up to you whether you want keep Adam close at bay or distant from you."

God had heard enough of the passion filled objections of Tree which was too potent for the king to endure. Growing rather annoyed by the sound of her voice which spewed flagrant opinions. Tree openness was quickly becoming the source of the king's displeasure. Unfurling the wrath of his anguish, God responded forcefully demanding Tree's obedience and silence. "Be still!" Demanded the king in a fierce and threatening tone. Tree was encouraged an end to her insolent behavior. The fierce warning gripped Tree with sobering fear and caused her nerves her to tremor and shake uncontrollably. Trembling frantically before her creator Tree exposed the very state of her nervousness and fear.

Tree honored her masters request and fell obediently silent. However, her involuntary compliance was imposed by the supernatural forces. God used his celestial powers to seal Tree's lips and remove her voice. Tree screamed and yelled out at the top of her lungs however the futile attempted was pointless. She attempted to communicate her complaints however was unable to produce the necessary sounds to carry her message forth. Tree's flaring spirit was unwilling to be silenced and subdued into submission. The pressure of oxygen surrounding Tree began to rapidly decrease. She was beginning to feel constricted and short of breath. Tree felt as though an invisible set of hands had somehow been placed over her face stopping her from taking in air." Tree fought back against the invisible forces that were attempting smother and suffocate her. In the present moment of crises, the absence of her voice became the least of her worries. Tree was now fighting for dear life clutching desperately to every pearl of breath she could muster. Even if Tree was able to speech, she would struggle to describe the constricting experience of being muzzled and gagged.

Tree could feel her heart racing, her nerves trembling uncontrollably in terror and suspense. Her frightened eyes began to fill, and overflow revealing the panic and fear she attempted to hide but was forced to disclose. God intentionally turned his back to Tree to display his indifference in the matter. His actions demonstrated a clear disregard and blatant dismissal of Tree's value and existence. No longer willing to accept any further treachery or contempt God punished Tree for her treasonous behavior.

Despite his stern exterior God was secretly masking his feeling behind his fiery temper and rage. God was unable to gaze directly into the face and eyes of his dearest companion and friend. Tree was being condemned and sentenced for perjury and treason as well as negligence in fulfilling her duties. "You insignificant and ungrateful log." The king hurled his abusive insults into the air. "I warned you about knowing your rightful place." God gestured disagreeably over the present state of Tree's present circumstances. "Your utility and service to Eden has been essential in maintaining and preserving life here in this wonderous garden. I admit you have helped to lavishly cultivate and transform Eden into a homely paradise. You have served your purpose well bringing forth beauty and splendor to this once barren world. Your natural ability to cultivate earth is why I have not extinguished or removed the flame of your essence and life force. I was able to overlook your many infractions and several acts of hubris treachery. It has become consequential that the height of your defiance has no limits or boundaries. I am sorry my dear friend, but I am left with only one resolution in dealing with disloyalty and betrayal."

Tree, struggled to free herself from the grips of defeat but found that she was unable to escape. The indistinguishable sound of muffled murmurs could be faintly heard. He watery eyes widened with desperation to convey sentiments that she could not communicate or express with words. "I am vaguely aware," God announced candidly.

"That you have a secret infatuation and admiration for man. I observed the preferential treatment and favor which you openly convey and demonstrate towards Adam. The question of your alliance has become transparently clear causing me to draw suspicion over your allegiance and guild." Tree was forced to listen to her master berate and belittle her character and name. "Since your return to Eden, you have grown to become quite careless and neglectful in carrying out your duties." God was attempting devalue and degrade Tree's worth by attacking her image. "You have grown much too comfortable, and noticeably enlarged in size and girth." God distastefully mocked Tree's hefty design playing on her natural appetite and zest for life. It was easy to see that Tree had become enormously thick and somewhat stout from the over consumption of rich and fertile soil. Hearing the berating and cruel words of her king's insults made Tree feel utterly betrayed and filled with disappointment. It was apparent that Tree had taken offense to God's insult her spirit heavily battered and bruised. Tree was filled with deep depression and sadness after hearing the unfiltered criticism of God's words.

It was no falsehood that Tree was no longer the youthful firmly shaped plant of her prime. However, the subject and matter of her bulk and size seemed more like a cheap jab than an observation. The superimposed insult was unnecessary and relatively insignificant to his point. God failed to consider the burdensome weight of responsibility Tree carried as the keeper of all living things. Tree had extended herself beyond the duties of her assignment. She managed to provide and care for multiple creatures and beings simultaneously. Tree was the resolver of conflicts as well as the keeper of many secretes. She serviced the needs of others by providing Eden with access to vegetation and produce necessary to sustain the inhabitants. In the present moment God was behaving just as arrogantly as his proud and self-righteous creations. The king was consumed by his ego and sense of entitlement. Had God taken a moment to look back at Tree's dreary face he would have found himself confronted by the image of sympathy and remorse. Tree's mournful disposition was enough to warrant a sympathetic pardon for her hubris transgressions.

Oddly enough God did not turn back to look at Tree. He found her stillness and silence to be delightfully rewarding to his ears. "You were supposed was to draw Adam closer to me!" God exclaimed. "By way of nudging subtle wisdom and endorsing my generosity and good grace. Instead, you have condoned and encouraged his profound and radical behavior to persist. You never once proposed that Adam relinquish his power and submit his will before my feet. Given direction Adam would have eventually learned to account for his wrongdoing and received my pardon and forgiveness. His call for penance and mercy would have easily demonstrated his commitment to fixing and mending our severed relationship."

God would have continued his passion filled ramblings if not disturbed by the muffled sound of pervasive laughter. His words had become a source of amusement and banter. The sound laughter annoyed the king as he turned to meet the face of his loathing agitator, "Do not mock my words!" God shouted boisterously, "You have no right to patronize me. I am his creator the source of all existence." Tree was unapologetically relentless confronted by her king's narcissism. The more God proclaimed his self-importance the more laughter seemed to fill the air. The powers of amusement and laughter helped to loosen the restraints of bondage that sealed and covered her mouth. Panting deeply and drawing heavy breaths Tree managed to break free of the enchanting spell. She heaved a heaping gust of air into her body and lungs before declaring passionately. "Adam, will never bow to you," Tree laughed mockingly. "See unlike the rest of the creatures in Eden, Adam does not fear you."

"It is true that man is not a god" Tree advanced further. "However, you fear that he will one day become godly in his own right. That is why you demand his allegiance and desire so desperately for him to join your cause. Adam will father civilization and in time his bloodline will abundantly multiply. The solidarity of man would only help to advance your agenda ensuring that you have at your disposal fleets of spiritual warriors devoted to your cause. Your inflated ego and selfish desire to source an unlimited supply of the precious love mineral will ultimately become your undoing. It saddens me to imagine the legion Adam's descendants tethered to the misguided belief that they are blessed and highly favored by their keeper. I pray for the lost lives of those pious souls who at the end of their earthly journey find themselves thrust into a celestial battlefront. You are unwittingly recruiting soldiers and warriors to fight in the unholy war being waged in the afterworld." God stood shockingly silent somewhat surprised and impressed by Tree's keen intuition and powers of deduction. "It has become plainly obvious as to why you designed this beautiful garden," Tree was stepping beyond the boundaries of her proper place. "Eden is conditioned to serve a perfect habitat and incubator operationally designed to encourage the fertility and procreation of life. You managed to stock this land with lively ammunition of countless souls whose only purpose is to serve your cause. Man exist solely as just another pawn another resource to help in your crusade of securing power and complete dictatorship."

God retained a stoic face of indignation drawing a smug grin over his face once again impressed by Tree's perceptive wit and intelligence. Tree's line of reasoning was condensed to include a broad spectrum of allegations intended to decipher and decode the king's intentions. She waited for God's admission and acknowledgement but strangely found her master unfazed or slighted in the least giving out a bellowing wave of laughter in response. "I am astonished," God responded casually. "That a ravishing mind such as yours can be so poorly equipped." God's backhanded compliment did not go unnoticed. "Imagine having such a complex and intricate plan unraveled by the likes of a simple-minded tree," God laughed out loudly, "I should have known better than to leave the task to Eve." Tree was surprised to hear God mention Eve's name suggesting her implication and involvement in the matter. Eve was being labeled an accessory to the current state of mischief and chaos.

"Eve and Abel's plan was masterful." God declared openly. "Much too intriguing and enticing for me to intervene or foil their scheme. Their actions though self-serving would help to severe Adam from his mate and rid him any potential distractions. They assumed that grief and loneliness would cause Adam to return home to Eden and ultimately back into their arms. The practicality of their dubious ploy garnered great success. Unfortunately, I could not circumvent the fatal exchange of misfortune and devastation that ensued as a consequence." God paused briefly as though conflicted by the thought of Abel's demise. He allowed a moment of silence to pass before speaking again.

"Oh well," God dismissed with a heavy sigh of indifference. "As far as Abel is concerned do not be sullied or saddened by his passing but rather be inspired by his death considering that he will be the first of many to set sights on the glory that is heaven." Tree had heard enough. She refused to accept the web of lies being spun and weaved before her eyes. She refused to yield or allow God to admonish his actions by ignoring his role in the destruction and death of Abel as well as Adam's mate. "I see now that Adam was right to leave this place." Tree sobbed tearfully with tears running down her face and body. "Who, or where can Adam be expected to turn after losing his beloved partner and mate. The single creature with whom he fostered an intimate bond and relationship is now dead. Adam is unable to console his anguished son Cain, now consumed with pain and hatred conflicted internally with bitterness and contention surrounding his father's betrayal. Do you expect that Adam will somehow turn to his vengeful father and creator whose occupational interests span beyond the confines of his private affairs. Just as Cain harbors feelings of bitterness and contempt towards his father so does Adam hold these same sentiments towards his creator. The cycle of civil unrest between father and son will only grow more contentious with each passing generation. Eventually this world will be filled with a host of unsupportive beings." Tree appeared depleted and out of breath. "It appears that mankind's fate is doomed to repeat the same self-serving story bound by the tradition of absenteeism. They will find means to justify their foundational desertion and neglect through the doctrines and actions of their predecessors and forefathers. The anchor of vigilance, and accountability which served to firmly ground man above the ranks of providence has been sadly unchained and misplaced. Many creators will choose to prioritize convenience over character and assume the somewhat godly role of an orbiting father figure who is remotely accessible."

Tree began to question the authenticity of Adams friendship and drawn-out relationship with Eve. She now suspected Eve's befriending and subtle seduction of Adam to be nothing more than a scripted rouse and sham to win his admiration, and affection. Tree was overcome with shame and embarrassment at the sudden revelation. She declared her solidarity and allegiance to Adam reinforcing and swearing candidly. "Adam will not lose faith in me!" She declared passionately. "I will offer him peace of mind by lifting the burden of guilt which he currently carries. I will unveil the web of lies and share with him the truth. The truth will help ease his tortured heart and mind from accepting responsibility for the tragic loss of his mate and child."

God was not amused by Tree's menacing threat to disclose the truth to Adam. Tree was an important figure helping to the keep the natural balance and order of the garden. Any other creature would have been quickly vanquished or removed but Tree's purpose was much too important to God's cause. Her natural duties were deeply rooted and entwined with maintaining and managing the upkeep and beauty of Eden, "I will reveal everything to Adam, " Tree warned with a tone of flagrant disdain and hostility etched in her voice, "I will make him aware of your involvement and let him know that it was Eve and Abel that conspired against his mate." Tree alluded to the threatening declaration before the watchful eyes and gaze of her impatient king."

God felt helpless growing rather uneasy against the weight and act of Tree's brazen defiance. "Do keep in mind that Adam can choose if he wishes to never return to Eden and to live out the rest of his days in exile and self-excommunication" God attempted pitifully to deflect and derail Tree's enthusiasm by offering her a less than appealing outlook and outcome to the present scenario. However, the king found little success in diminishing the flaring spirit of Tree's defiant protest. "Oh, he will be back," Tree answered with absolute certainty. "And when he does arrive seeking consoling, I will be sure to offer him counsel and remove the burden of guilt and grief weighing over his shoulders. I will cast away the cloud of gloom and despair that hovers above him granting him the truthful answers to his questions and inquiries."

God was growing rather annoyed if not irritated with Tree's rebellious behavior. She carried a vested sense interest in wanting to disclose and reveal the contemptuous plan set to sabotage Adam. "When Adam arrives baring his troubles, I will lighten his load by reassuring him that these unfortunate circumstances were not of his own doing, and that the burden of guilt and despair should not be his to carry alone. I will encourage that he redirects his frustrations at his conniving and selfish creator who plotted and conspired against him. Employing Eve and Abel as pawns and minions to serve out your will and bidding." Tree paused a moment before approaching the pinnacle of an overwhelming thought.

"I cannot imagine that it was easy for you." Tree began again this time speaking softly. "Or any creator for that matter to watch their creation live a fulfilling and happy life entirely independent and void of their fathers help. Why then would you foolishly embed within the core fabric or your creation self-determination and free will." "Wait, unless." Tree began to speculate. "The qualifying attribute was made in err as a compromising flaw. It is impossible to fathom that any fault could occur at the hands of a perfect creator who openly declares to never making errors or mistakes." Tree seemed to mock and laughed openly at the king. "Adam would have served you well in you purpose had you given him the half the chance instead of being consumed by his limits and shortcomings. And had you committed a fraction of your time and energy into Adam's rearing rather than at his ensnaring the crises of unfortunate events could have possibly been averted."

The king was outraged by Tree's proclamation and struggled to contain his temper. "You may be right." God responded grimly, "However I cannot allow you to reveal such profound secrets to Adam. His allegiance to the cause is much too vital and important in fulfilling my masterful plan." The subtle change in the king's hostile tone hinted that something unsavory was looming. "The outcome of my plan is dependent on Adams compliance and commitment. I will not allow you or any creature to risk or jeopardize my plans. For this reason, I have decided that upon my departure from Eden I will be taking with me your voice and thus removing your natural ability to speak and communicate with Adam or any creature in the garden. I cannot risk you disclosing an accounting of my disingenuous deeds. The relinquishment will extend beyond the capability of speech, you will be made mute no longer able to utter a sound or speak out."

"No please!" Tree cried out painfully as though afflicted by the charge of her censorship "Yes!" God answered offering a quick rebuttal. "You will no longer be able to speak to Adam for I fear that you know far too much. Had it not been for Adam's and the sake of arousing suspicion I would have conveniently relocated you to the furthest area of the nether regions. The imposing sanctions will ultimately relinquish your ability and powers to orate and propagate. The sound of your voice will forever be silenced as you will no longer harness the skill set of speech. You will exist only to serve and fulfill your ground keeping duties that is to maintain and sustain Eden." The king paused with a widening smirk amused by the thought that appeared suddenly to him,

"Ironically this sentencing will force you to confront your archenemies." God stopped abruptly in a deliberate effort to build climatic suspense. He waited for the look of confusion to glaze over Tree's face and creased brows. "Silence!" God blurted out suddenly in a taunting display of mockery and laughter. The tactless gesture only helped to demonstrate the kings dark and somewhat dry sense of humor. God vanished suddenly disappearing just as effortlessly as he appeared leaving only the lingering sounds of his laughter echoing through the air. Tree tried to speak out but found that she could not muster a sound. She tried over and over repeatedly yelling obsessively but found herself unable to break free of the silent spell.

Meanwhile on the other side of Eden Eve was in state of mourning after burying her only child resting his body underneath a bed of blooming flowers. She reserved the hopes that her son's spirit would continue to somehow live existing on in the stems, petals and roots and of all the beautiful delicate flowers. Eve was truly gifted with a knack for vision and imagination. She managed to multiply beauty and splendor in everything she touched. Eve offered her deceased son a glorious and wonderful eulogy and send off commiserating the tragic and unfortunate loss of Abel's life.

After holding vigil Eve wandered about aimlessly engrossed in the private conversation and discourse occurring in her mind. Eve carried a heavy sense of remorse and guilt for her role in of Abel's death. She held private council contemplating deeply over the senseless deed. The prejudice of moral inventory became evident as Eve struggled on whether she should confess her wrongdoing. "If my love for Adam is honest, and true than I must confess the truth to him." Eve demonstrated her ambivalence by professing her declarations, and afterward retracting the very notion. She felt emotionally conflicted and overwhelmed by the burden and weight of her present circumstances. "But how can I tell Adam, without implicating myself in the admission."

Eve began to hesitate and re-exam her views more carefully after finding plausible faults in every possible scenario. She was consumed with torment and filled with bitterness and regret along with a host of unflattering thoughts. Eve wrestled with the idea omitting her involvement but dismissed the thought as another form of deceit. She made up her mind unable to accept the burden and shame of guilt weighing over her. At the first sight and opportunity Eve planned to confess the truth to Adam offering clarity to the events which led to death and demise of Abel and his mate. She intended afterward to plea and beg for his mercy and forgiveness with the hope that he would view the noble act of her confession as a redeeming quality. "I will prove to him that my love is true and earn back his trust."

Eve walked away sluggishly from Abel's burial site, headed back towards the direction garden. She felt smothered beneath a tidal wave of daunting feelings. The fresh wounds of grief unhinged ghastly emotions by the imposing sentimental images and memories of Abel into her mind. The haunting thought of Abel's stiff body appeared suddenly in her mind. The intrusive thoughts provoked tears to flood down her eyes and face. Eve collapsed suddenly to the ground falling on her knees and began sobbing uncontrollably "What have I done!" She cried out in loathsome desperation and self-pity.

"Greetings'Sss, my queen?" Declared an unfamiliar voice echoing from deep within in the tumble bushes. "Who is there?" Eve demanded to know. "Who are you. Reveal yourself to me." Suddenly a strange creature appeared from the bushes slithering slowly out into the open. Eve was startled and somewhat intrigued by the lengthy serpent creature. "My Apologies'Sss. I did not mean to startle you. I am Snake," hissed the stranger. "It is an honor to finally meet you." Eve stopped to observe the visitor closely but could not deduce any recollection of having met or encountered the legless creature in the garden before this day, "I have often observed you during your strolls through in the garden. However, you have never been low enough to the ground to become formally acquainted." Snake spoke with enchanting politeness as he slithered gracefully closer to Eve.

"My condolences'Sss' to you regarding the sudden and unfortunate loss of your son and our prince." Snake offered his regard, "I was peacefully passing by when I was drawn by the commotion of your sorrowful outcry. In overhearing the source of your troubles, I was moved if not compelled to provide you wisdom and guidance suggesting that you not confess'Sss' those horrid truths to Adam." Eve was shockingly embarrassed and blushed at her carelessness. She remained silent and tamed uncertain as to the appropriate reaction and response. "You simply mustn't my dear," Snake advised with reassured guidance. "Unveiling such truths to Adam will hinder your agenda and only help to sow seeds of distrust and contempt towards you. The secret that you bring to him will only ignite anguish and outrage within him. The knowledge of your involvement in the destruction of his family will only further the separation and divide between Adam and yourself. The shattering discovery which you intend to disclose will surely send Adam spiraling into madness and lunacy."

Eve stood considerably silent listening to Snake as he provided a less than optimistic point of view. The clarity of his perception caused Eve to reconsider the full weight and gravity of her current circumstance. "What should I do?" Eve cried pleading desperately for guidance and reassurance "I have nowhere and no one with whom to turn. My closest friend only child is now dead because of me. And it is all my fault." Eve cried out hysterically overwhelmed by sadness and grief. The wounding loss of her son was still fresh in her mind causing her strife and pain and other symptoms associated with grief. Eve was brought to tears by the sudden thought and image of her son that seem to appear and surface suddenly into her mind"

"Do not be stifled by the loss'Sss' of your child my dear queen," Snake assured Eve. "Prince Abel has passed on from this would however there is still hope." Eve looked queerly at Snake with growing regard and interest, "God is'Sss' good," Snake declared. "He can bring back Abel back you to you and can bless you abundantly with many more children." Eve felt rejoiced by the idea and thought of having Abel back in her arms recalling the soothing warmth of her sons embrace which she had already began to miss. "Working together you, and I along with God can assure that Adam returns'Sss home permanently." Eve looked strangely at Snake with a glare of suspicion in her eyes. "I do not understand." Eve answered still somewhat confused and uncertain as to Snake's relation and association to the king. "What do you mean." Eve inquired. "Who are you?" Come now my queen," Snake hissed passively. "Who I am is of no significance consider me like yourself a humble serpent,… I mean servant of our loyal creator and shepherd." Eve felt a strange sense overwhelming familiarity in the presence of the unknown and mysterious guest. His elusive and shifty demeanor was evidenced by his deliberate attempt to disregard and evade her prior inquiry. "Do you honestly, believe that Adam will forgive you? Or have you so easily forgotten your pivotal role and involvement in the vicious ploy to butcher his mate which in effect caused the death and demise of his son." Eve was hurt emotionally in having been hit by the blunt objectivity of truth in Snakes harsh message.

"Have you forgotten your morning prayer in which you called to our king to help fulfill your devious plot. "God, pleases keep my son Abel safe in his travels." "That was your solemn request, correct." Snake patronized. "And who do you believe it was that produced the thick mist and fog which allowed Abel to travel and navigate in stealth beneath the cloak of the blinding fog." Eve was stricken with shock. "But how do you know all this." She was growing impatiently short tempered and unamused by her provocative guest. Snake would not answer or respond directly to Eve's but instead encouraged her to heed his advice and consider his council. "My dear Eve," Snake addressed Eve casually as though the two had been historically acquainted before this introduction.

Slithering slowly and drawing closer to Eve. He stopped and raised his body up so that their faces would meet. Peering directly into Eve's eyes he spoke, "The last I checked you are I are the only creature in this garden in possession and guard of this unspeakable secret." Eve seemed annoyed and somewhat insulted by Snake's alluding invitation to collude and conspire. "Great, more secrets,' Eve gestured her indignation by throwing her hands madly into the air and back down again. She appeared exhausted if not annoyed of by the pretense of Snakes rhetoric's. Eve was becoming rather weary of the intentions of the shifty visitor, and the direction of their engagement. The unsavory character seemed rather intense in his attempt to persuade Eve to refrain her disclosure. "No!" Eve responded defiantly. "I cannot." Her ambivalent demeanor demonstrated an internal conflict waring within her mind and subconscious. "I do not care to discuss this matter any further." Eve was clear in her declaration and unwillingness to participate or entertain the discussion of civil conspiracy. Eve was prepared to bring an end to the cycle of lies by dispelling the truth.

The contempt of serving as an accessory and accomplice in the completion of filicide loitered irredeemably in her mind. "It is true." Eve declared somberly. "That Adam may never forgive me for what I have done." Eve was conflicted with her feuding emotions. She found herself feeling once again divided and torn uncertain which path she should follow. The worthy adversary who upon observing Eve's moment of vulnerability and hesitation began applying pressure. Snake strongly encouraged Eve to consider the consequences of her action opposed to her inaction. Eve was metaphorically allowing herself to be pinned into submission by Snake's mongering line of reasoning. Eve sat stoic and motionless in deep thought processing the short list of viable options remaining. It did not take long before Eve became annoyed and irritated demonstrating her submission with an exhausting sigh and a dramatic drop of her shoulder to signify her surrender and overwhelming defeat.

At witnessing Eve's submission Snake began to draw excitement and pursued further, "Do not be upset my queen," Snake reassured. "Instead think of this secret as an opportunity to win favor from our master. Let this secret serve as an irrevocable ledger and pact forged between God and yourself. In time this secret alliance will garner favor over your bloodline strengthening their bond and allegiance with our king. You will reap abundantly and be blessed with grace and great favor. If kept unspoken this secret has the potential to secure you substantial leverage and rank over Adam viewing, you as God most prized creature. For your unwavering obedience in keeping this oath of secrecy God will reward you by catering to you and your many descendants. You will forever be admired and celebrated as the mother of civilization. God will aspire to form and replicate more beings like yourself in an effort to duplicate the same quality of devotion." Snake's prophecy was remarkably detailed and enticing for Eve who was now in deep thought and contemplation.

"Do not worry yourself my queen," Snake reassured Eve. "For God will never attempt to recount your secret or impose on the boundaries of your relationship if you remain eternally faithful to our king. Do not reveal or expose Adam to the clandestine meeting that has taken place today. If you are loyal and prudent in retaining our masters love and trust. He will one day grant you a royal throne beside him in the kingdom of heaven. There you will be reunited with your son, and reign forever side by side as the prince and queen of the royal heavens."

Snake's enticing proposal was impossible to dismiss or ignore. The offer held a great amount of appeal and attraction that worked slowly to restore hope and optimism about the future. She began to draw rejuvenation from the joyful imagines and thoughts of an illustrious and fulfilling life in heaven. Eve like many creatures at the time believed heaven to be a most wonderful and magnificent place. The massive beauty of heaven was tenfold more spectacular than that of the Eden. The thought of being reunited with her son and seeing Abel's tender face filled Eve's heart and spirit with happiness. Just as quickly as the warm sentiments emerged the feeling subsided even quicker. The moment was brief and short lived as Eve was now faced with the truthful realization of her sorrowful state and present circumstances.

"I see that you are in deep thought and contemplation." Snake regarded. "And as so I will leave you to your imagination. But I bid you to consider the unfathomable wealth, and favor you stand to gain. This entire world could become yours if you are able to conceal your secret from Adam." And just like that without another word shared Snake took his leave slithering back into the tumble bushes from whence he emerged. Eve did not respond but stood frozen in silence. She leveraged the possibilities of reasonable outcomes that played over in her mind. Suddenly, without warning Eve gave a startling scream before placing her face into her palms. She began to weep and cry out inconsolably. Unknowingly to Eve on the other side of the land Adam too was crying mournfully before the body of his beloved mate.

12

The Confrontation

Adam sat weeping before the lifeless body of his beloved mate, "I am so sorry." He cried out. "I did not mean to bring such a cursed end to your life. I never imagined that this would be the outcome of your fate." Cain stood in the shadowy corner of his cavern nursing his anguish and quaking nerves. He wanted to strike his father with a blow but found that he could not muster up the will to perform the dreadful act. Hearing Adam's constant apologies to his departed mother served as an affront to Cain that only intensified his growing desire to react belligerently. "Why God!" He wallowed tearfully. "This should not be." He gripped his mate tightly consoling the lifeless body of his partner.

Despite the swelling tension Cain remained reserved, and self-contained in his demeanor exercising a great deal of restraint. Lingering quietly in the shadows Cain listened closely to his father's sorrowful ramblings and in hearing his woeful admissions it became clear his father's sins and transgressions. Hearing Adam call out and acknowledge the very name of God was distressing if not triggering. The name God rang in Cain's ears like an irritating sound that pained his nerves, He recalled having heard the name of God mentioned by Tree in relation to his mother death. "Who is God?" Cain demanded to know breaking his silence.

"God is my father and also my creator," Adam answered, "He is also your grandfather." Cain seem unmoved by Adam's admission and regarded the declaration with skepticism and indifference. "God is the creator of all that exist. Adam continued. "God is the developer and architect of all that we see and all that surround us." Cain seemed vexed at his father's response, sensing a hint of admiration and regard in Adam's description of God. Cain began to grow irritated looking around at the hardened structure and dry stoned interior of their home, "Look around us father!" Cain rebelled, "Look at all of this degradation and darkness surrounding us. Before today I had never believed or known that there existed such a bountiful and wondrous paradise. Had it been I who discovered Eden I would have carried word and placed our family into more comfortable conditions." Adam shook his head with annoyance already forecasting the direction of Cain's weathering words.

"The land of Eden is an abundantly vast estate." Cain declared. "Large enough for us to inhabit and share the communal spacing. Eden could have easily accommodated lodging for two families to inhabit and call and home. But instead, you chose to leave mother and I in this deplorable state. We were forced to accept shelter within the bowls of a mountain surrounded by bedrock and stony debris. While you pursue a carefree and enchanted life with the hopes of nurturing a second family and household." Cain stopped abruptly pausing to choose his next set of words carefully. "You are a selfish man father." Cain denounced with deliberate disregard and contempt for his father, "You are a lowly figure who belongs rightfully beneath the putrid rocks." Adam felt violated taking immediate offense to the wrath of tailored insults, "I bid you restrain your tongue and check your next few words carefully. Do not forget even in your tempered state that I am still your father and creator thus rightfully due my respect." Adam appeared equally outraged by Cain's conduct and condemning tone.

The prowling look drawn over Adam's face was fierce and intense. The ferocious gaze was enough to ward off any agitator, however it failed to repel his son. Cain was hardly moved by the fraudulent expressions of his father, "Lo, and behold," Cain mocked. "So, it is you who are the God of me now?" The patronizing words of Cain seemed to bruise Adam's delicate ego. The moment of insincerity dawned over Adam as he listened to his son's belittling remarks. Adam experienced a moment of nostalgia recalling the countless times when he as youth hurled similar insults to deface and defile his father and creator.

In an ironic turn of fate Adam found himself on the receiving end of his son's bellowing gripes. The unnatural onslaught of criticism received from Cain only helped to further irritate and annoy Adam. The disgraceful and slanderous insults being hurled at him by his son began to unravel and reshape his beliefs "Is this the destiny of man?" Adam questioned. "To inherit the scolding embers of hatred, and resentment from one father to another. I can no longer deny the glorious divine power of our creator God. He instilled in every creature the breath and the gift of life." Adam became remorseful for his son, urging Cain to submit, "Please my son" Adam plead openly. "I cannot bear the burden of having to lose or bury another child." Adam began to sob uncontrollably before the feet of his son.

Cain stood silently over his father glowing with anguish and bitter contempt. The image of witnessing his hero and champion crying and sulking pitifully like a child was a disenchanting image that seemed to fill Cain with disgust and disappointment. He was now viewing Adam through the lens of a senseless old man. Cain began to feel somber and somewhat remorseful reflecting over the unintentional life he had just taken. A nagging suspicion began to form in Cain's mind hindering his beliefs. "Who was that boy," Cain posed the question to his father but he did not receive a response from Adam. "Answer me, who was he!" Cain demanded in a fierce and intimidating tone. Cain was beginning to grow rather annoyed and irritated by his father's reluctance to respond. Adam sensing the growing tension in Cain's tone offered to provide his son some words of comfort to pacify and resolve his growing angst. "Why seek answers to questions that no longer concern you." Adam answered rhetorically, "What does it matter now that he is dead."

Adam's response was vague his intention to evoke sympathy and remorse from Cain who seemed unapologetic and defensive for what he had done. "I did not kill him!" Cain pleaded in a passionate rebuttable. "He exchanged his life for that of his mothers." Cain stopped suddenly as if arrested by the sound of his own words, "It was a noble act." He stated hesitantly. "A life for a life is a most befitting and honorable exchange." Adam was wrought with despair shocked at hearing the complexity of Cain's admission. It appeared that his son was uneasy and somewhat distraught harboring a small fraction of remorse for having accidentally slain his own brother.

"I would have happily done the same had I been present during mothers attack." The unbridled truths of Cain's words drew awkwardness and silence between the two. Adam did not have a doubt in his mind that Cain adored his mother and would have happily laid down his own life in the same exchange and manner. It was with that sudden realization Adam felt convicted to share with his son some priceless words and gems of wisdom, "You are my son." Adam declared. "And as your father I am obligated to guide if not prepare you for your journey thru life." Cain seemed annoyed by the very sound of his father's voice and scoffed at the offer of reconciliation with arrogant disdain. "We are cursed." Adam began. "To live, and struggle against the nature of our design. The illusion of happiness never seems to last for creatures like us. I fear that one day you too shall indulge in the bittersweet nectar and fruit that is life. And when this day arrives, it is my hope that you assume a port better than myself. Do not allow the soft pedals of desire, and temptation to run ramped and assume priority over your virtue." Adams words were heavy and strikingly blunt leaving Cain somewhat baffled and confused by his father's rhetoric. "Cursed!" Cain mocked spitefully with laughter while secretly internalizing the emotions that surfaced after hearing his father brazen proposals. Adam's loaded warnings yielded unlimited potential and shed light to answers and questions never spoken between the two. "I don't understand father, why are we cursed? What wrongful sin have we committed to receive such cruel judgment."

Cain found himself peaking attentively with interest waiting for a response from his father, but Adam answered with muted silence. The uncomfortable moment drew an air of awkwardness between the two. The smothering tension between father, and son was becoming unbearably thick and rather unsettling "It was God." Cain cried out suddenly. 'Who sent your son to slay my mother." "No, my son." Adam refused to accept. "You are sadly mistaken and confused if you believe that God summoned Abel to commit such a heinous act." Adam pleaded desperately for Cain's understanding and placed his arms gently on his son's shoulders. "I do not fully understand why or what drove Abel to commit such a terrible sin." Adam began to feel an inflating sense of guilt swelling inside him. He paused suddenly as if overcome by a sudden revelation. He considered the impact and frequency of his absence and remote presence in both his family's lives. In hindsight Adam was able to clearly view the conflict of his dueled role and decision. He accepted accountability for his parental neglect and was highly critical of his failed role as a devoted protector and provider. Adam blamed and scolded himself for the unfortunate demise and death of his mate and child. He held himself in contempt for the oversight of regard and commitment shown to his late partner and son. Adam was conflicted with the delusional and irrational belief that he not been attentive to the care and needs of his mate and son. The burden of guilt caused Adam to look back and reflect in search of clues. He replayed images in his mind searching for subtle signs of distress. He examined Abel's behavior for abnormal behavior anything that should have served as an indication or caused alarm. Adam could not recall any behavioral patterns or troubling signs that would explain the senseless act of violence.

Cain took offense to his father attempt at excusing the deplorable actions of his murderous son. He was outraged and upset by Adam's posturing campaign of defense. "Why won't you accept the truth!" Cain yelled out defiantly growing rather annoyed with his father. "How can you defend the murderer of my mother after what he has done. He singlehandedly destroyed our family and home And yet you still refer to him as your son." Cain appeared irritated and disappointed. "He killed my mother!" Cain cried out passionately with swelling tears streaming down his frustrated and anguished face. Adam did not answer and instead chose to ignore his son's statement disregarding the need to respond or explain. Hovering over Adam who was still crouched down on the ground consoling his mate. It became painfully obvious and clear that Adam was presently in a lowly plight and station. His unwillingness to relinquish Abel's title and kinship was perceived as dishonorable by Cain who deemed the scornful gesture as inexcusable. Adam could sense the heat radiating from his tempered and outraged son. He accepted that the tormented creature standing before him was not his son. The Cain he knew and raised was a naturally kind and loving creature. The tragic loss of his mother was impactful and partly transformative as Cain struggled to navigate the emotional hurdles of misery and sorrow. He was clouded in his judgment overly consumed by pain and grief. The once kind and gentle being was gradually transforming into a hardened and cynical creature.

"Abel's actions do not reflect the will of God," Adam attempted to explain to his irritated and annoyed son. "I will not deny that God is an unreliable father however, he is a just and fair king as I have come to discover. But only if you surrender your will and allow him to command your life. He will support and watch over you assuring that you prosper and live abundantly." Cain was astonished and looked on at his father as though he was a headless being with four arms. He could no longer stand the sight of his father and was unwilling to listen to any more of Adams berserk ramblings about fatherhood and God. however, he did not attempt to interrupt.

"You see son," Adam began again. "You and I are one in the same. We are special beings' uniquely different from all the other creations. We are the only creatures blessed and gifted with full autonomy and free will." "Free will," Cain mocked as though unbelieving of his father words. "Yes," Adam advanced. "We are free from the limitations imposed upon other creatures of the world. We are exempt from principals and laws which confine and limit other creatures. As man we are permitted to choose the course and direction of our own lives. God has granted us this liberty and freedom to do as we see fit." Adam voice turned sorrowful, "It is only when I began to stray from his grace that misfortune and tragedy began to assume and plague my life. It is not wise to fight against the will of your father as I have come to accept having wasted so much time in doing so. I hope that you avoid my path and come to accept God as your lord and savior sooner than myself. Submit yourself now to God's divine will and pray for his forgiveness so that you may be forgiven and absolved of your sins"

Cain was now gravely infuriated at his father's petition. "I was like you once." Adam continued. "Rebellious and difficult to control. I would not adhere to the cautionary warnings, or council of others." Cain was now fed up. He could no longer stomach the senseless garbage spewing from his father lips., "Oh please father." Cain interrupted unapologetically. He was unwilling to endure another moment of his father spiritual rhetoric's. "I am now fully convinced that you have truly lost your wits and plunged into madness." The jabbing insult was painfully hurtful serving as an affront which bruised Adam's ego and punctured his heart. Overlooking the offence Adam chose to excuse and pardon Cain for his childish outburst and behavior. "How can you say that God is good," Cain raged angerly. "When he is responsible for the death of your mate and my mother." "God, is anything, but good!" Cain yelled out with extreme prejudice and defiance as though extremely annoyed by his father remarks.

Adam could feel the heat of Cain's eyes peering down over him. He could feel heat of his fiery gaze beaming down against his neck and backside. "To live a long prosperous life." Adam counseled. "Man must first learn how to forgive the most wicked and vilest of offenders, be it themself." Cain paused at hearing his father's remark but was still unsure at to what to make of his father present state of mind and judgment. "It makes no sense." Adam continued. "To point and place the blame on God, when in fact this tragedy is due to my own conduct and neglect. The spirit of God flows through me just as it runs through you. This divine connection is what drives our insatiable hunger and pursuit for greatness. The monolithic desire to become all-knowing and all-powerful like our mighty creator and master is what binds us. I find that we are cursed in the active pursuit of unattainable goals. It was baseless to pursue the dream of becoming omnipotent and somewhat god like. The remanence of God's love is embedded within all his creatures guiding them into their natural order and purpose. However, as man we seek to forge our own path and tread our own course in search of meaning and purpose. Our downfall and inherent misfortune lays in our desire to become omniscient and omnipresent. You are right son; man cannot exist in two places at once however the desire still exists.

The moment of awkward silence began to resurface between father and son. "You my son carry within you the insatiable hunger for greatness. The desire to exceed God's limitations and boundaries lives dormant within us. This is the curse of man!" Adam exclaimed, "I have suffered the ravenous affliction of depravation and neglect just as your children and their heirs will soon experience." Cain was appalled if not offended by at his father's declaration. "Two places at once." Cain repeated absurdly. "Father at first, I was uncertain as to the state of your mental health and condition. However now am now convinced that you have lost grip of your sanity." Cain laughed out loud kneeling over his father. The taunting sound of Cain's laughter echoed throughout the room. The cackle offered little amusement and only helped to further infuriate Adam's flaring temper. "Do not mock me!" Adam raged before the presence of his insolent son. The outburst rang loudly throughout the cavern walls alerting Cain to fact that he had crossed a personal boundary. Adam slowly lifted himself from the ground onto his feet and was now staring directly into face of his son. The icy glare over Cain's face displayed the burden of anguish and frustration he harbored.

Cain stood defiantly before his father with frowned faced and beaten brow. He did not shy away or back down from the optical performance of intimidation. An intense stare down ensued between the two titans that lasted for an uncomfortably long time. Cain struggled against the intensity of his father's gaze overcome with swelling tension and anxiety. His nerves trembled violently as he braced himself to receive a fierce blow from his father. He accepted the preemptive attack with heightened anticipation. In his mind the assault would justify his call to protect and defend himself. It would be then that Cain would unleash the fury of his wrath and anguish onto his father.

Adam did not react impulsively or resort to barbaric conduct. Instead, he leaned closer to his opposition with only inches separating their faces. In a chilling face-off Adam spoke firmly. "I am quite sane son.' Adam whispered into Cain's ear. "Do you want to know who killed your mother? "Adam teased rhetorically, and without waiting for an answer he responded, "It was me." Adam expressed open heartedly. "I killed your mother." The shocking confession threw Cain off his pivot causing him to take a few steps back. Cain stood motionless and terror stricken crippled with fear to the point that he could hardly breath or speak. Adam could see that his son was taken aback by the loaded admission. He felt compelled to explain and provide clarity and context to his words. "No," Adam affirmed. "I did not strike the fatal blow that ended your mother's life, but I am somewhat responsible for the fatal outcome."

"If you allow me." Adam humbled himself. "I will share with you the entire story and tale of my existence. I am willing to answer any if not all of your questions after my conclusion." Cain did not respond feeling somewhat baffled by the grief-stricken generosity of his father. Cain was impressionably unsettled feeling deflated by the absence of reasoning. He seemed desperate in his search for understanding and reasoning. "I can explain." Adam offered to share. "Why this misfortune is partly, if not solely my fault." Cain did not respond but waited patiently for Adam to begin his explanation. "God wanted to take me away from you and your mother." Adam began. "He wanted me to stay inside Eden, and live as he had intended for life. God went as far as to conjure up and design a mate similar toy your mother's creed and likeness. The creature possessed beauty, and charm, but no amount of beauty or charm could keep me away from your mother and my family. I loved your mother dearly; however, I sinned and fell short in my lustful ambitions. I allowed the curse of man to consume and overtake me." Adam regarded. "I desired to exist in two places at once; I wished to possess Eve and still retain the love and affection of your mother. In hindsight I can see how foolish my lofty agenda and goals now appear."

Cain could not believe what he was witnessing after hearing the heartfelt confessions of his father. Despite the dreariness of Adam's declaration his words resonated truth and honesty in his tone. The tender bond of antiquity shared between Adam and Cain was brief, yet the moment of allowed for vulnerability and transparency between father and son. Cain was intrigued if not drawn to his discretionary words. "The act was selfish on my part." Adam admitted. "However, at the time I was young, wild and untamed. The very creature Eve, who you attempted to slay appeared suddenly becoming a distraction that piqued my interest and curiosity. Eve offered me an escape from the menial and mundane life that I had become grossly accustomed. The nature of her seduction was gracefully adorned in youthful splendor and beauty. She was remarkably tailored seemingly absent of any imperfections or flaws." Adam paused dropping his head pitifully to the floor before placing his hands onto Cain shoulder,

"I have fallen short." Adam explained accepting accountability, "I allowed my growing lust, and untamed emotions to consume and blind me. I let myself be spellbound and subdued by a foreign enchantress. I was overly smitten with attraction and deliberately placed myself in the troughs of sin and seduction. I understood clearly that Eve was created to serve as a wedge of division between your mother and myself. However, by the time I realized what was happening it was too late. The gentle seed of life had already been sown and could not be undone. I am sorry son and extend my deepest condolences and sympathies to your mother who I loved and adored dearly."

Cain seem unmoved by Adam's explanation seeing as the excuse made for a lousy defense. He was in no way persuaded or convinced by his father's forlorn and pathetic attempt. "The creature Eve soon bore us a child. Abel the young man who you encountered and accidently slayed was indeed your brother. "My brother?" Cain repeated questionably as though surprised by the discovery. "Yes," Adam answered, "He is your half-brother, having entered through this world through the same spiritual outlet and channels. Abel was a kind and gentle boy who I never imagined was filled with anguish, and bitterness festering deep within him. I never could not foresee that envy, and jealousy would drive him to commit such an unforgiving and heinous act." Adam gazed despairingly at the cold lifeless body of his deceased partner and mate. Looking into the face of his mate Adam became instantly filled overwhelming grief and sadness. He seemed to buckle beneath the intense weight of sadness burling over him. Suddenly without provocation or any instigation Adam broke down and began tearfully whimpering and crying hysterically like a child.

"I am so sorry," Adam cried out to the lifeless body of his mate. "I was your mate and partner." Adam sobbed tearfully. "I was responsible if not accountable for your life, but I failed you." Adam whimpered and wailed blaming himself for his partners death and no one else. "Look what I allowed to happen to you my dear and what I let happens to us." Tears began to flow from Cain's eyes after witnessing the melancholy sentiments of sadness of his father. The powerful image evoked feelings of dread and sorrow that resonated perfectly with the mournful occasion. The heartfelt admission that preceded just moments earlier revealed the irksome truth that Cain had indeed slain his own brother. The irony reflected on the fact that Cain had always wanted a younger brother and sibling to befriend and call his own. Cain recalled the botched efforts of his parents in attempting to provide him with a younger sibling and remembering the premature, and fatal miscarriages that served as a dark cloud over their lives. Adam and his mate after countless failed attempts at conceiving decided it best to postpone the idea of an additional child for the moment. The couple intended to revisit the idea again in the future but due to unforeseen circumstances of his mother's demise Cain would never receive a younger sibling.

The combination of his guilt and shame weighed heavily over his conscious tormenting his heart and mind. Cain's thoughts raced frantically "He was my brother." Cain echoed silently beneath his breath confronted by the startling revelation of kinship. "Abel was my brother!" Cain shouted. "You mean to tell me that all this time the bitter void of loneliness that haunted me was unwarranted and without purpose. Had I known or been aware of my brother's existence in the least. I would have gladly made acquaintances of him. Our union and friendship could have helped to remove the dormant feelings of emptiness and loneliness that I harbored during your absences." "It is not that simple," Adam interrupted. "No father!" Cain fired back. "It is that simple. Did you not just confess that we were designed of free will." "Yes." Adam agreed uncertain as to Cain's point. "Then why did you not bring us together rather than allowing me to unknowingly slay my brother."

The chilling truth of Cain's words caused Adam to fall into freezing bitter silence, Adam found himself wrestling against his thoughts. He began to conceptualize alternative outcomes to the fatal loss of his mate. Adam entertained various conclusions to his predicament that were absent of fatalities. He questioned and pondered over whether the death of his mate and son could have avoided. Adam dwelled silently in deep thought possibly regretting some decisions that he made. "Can you not see father." Cain stated openly. "That God has discovered man's weakness and is attempting to exploit and take advantage of this vulnerability." Adam seemed baffled and somewhat confused by the idea that his son was attempting to covey and promote. "The curse of man," Cain continued. "Is nothing more than the seduction of the flesh." Adam looked up at his son as though astounded by the validity of truth behind his bold declaration. "You fell short admittedly in the face of temptation once before, and I fear that if you return back to Eden, Father you will surely fall again."

Standing inches away from his father Cain and Adam were separated by the body and corpse of their dearly beloved lying on the ground. "Do you not see son." Adam returned. "That is exactly my point. Why do we rebel against our creator when he is our father and wants only what is best for his children." Cain looked contemptuously at his father as though baffled by Adams senseless rhetoric. Adam turned his attention over to his mate. "God cautioned and forbade me to pursue after your mother. However, I rebelled and refused to obey his command. In the end the tragic outcome of misfortune and misery would be issued as a result of my defiance." Adam mirrored the gaze of tension and frustration towards his son. "Had I heeded my father's warning and obeyed God's commands as doctrines of truth. I would be assuming the port of my ordained role and destiny beside my creator and father." Adam with preceding allegiance appeared committed to fulfilling the pious cause. "By this time alone, I would have occupied my position and seat as the rightful prince of the heaven; ruling over this world and many more like it."

"Believe me son." Adam confessed openly. "I loved your mother dearly. Our introduction caused a sudden a change to take place within me. The emotional transformation crippled my inhibitions and increased my sense of honor and duty. I became more engrossed in the calling of fatherhood and provider-ship; possibly losing myself in the process of it all. I was attracted to the notion of curating my own path believing that it would lead to a new and unexplored life. I willingly subscribed to the idea that your mother and I could create our own way together as a united family. Sadly, the challenge proved much more difficult than initially anticipated. I learned shortly after your birth that raising a family was no easy feat, but rather a weary and toilsome task. Often your mother and I felt entrapped, and ensnared like the very beasts that we hunted, and preyed after. For the first time in my existence, I became solemnly aware that I was no longer the master of my free will. Like a marionette threaded by the capricious hands of a master puppeteer. I found myself being enveloped within the role and station assigned to me by generous hands of fate and destiny. I was hurled between the dutiful role of honor and indentured servitude. Each assignment was prescriptively different yet identical in obligation and practice."

"You may not recall." Adam reasoned. "Because you were either too young, or simply refuse to remember it." Cain could not believe his ears listening to the sullied words of his absent-minded father. The thought and ideas described by Adam helped to further the flawed image of his character before the eyes of his son. It was without saying that Adams character and reputation was seriously at jeopardy. He was facing the emotional tribunal occurring in his head. The remainder of pilers and monuments which Cain erected in his mind to honor his father began to chip away and crumble collapsing before his very eyes. The faltering remains of his valiance and bravery were now covered in debris. Adam stood before Cain as a symbol of wrought and degradation for having allowed himself to fall so far from grace. Adam saw no use in trying to explain the dynamic complexities of child rearing to one who was unfamiliar and still inexperienced. "You do not understand." Adam woefully protested. "Because you have yet to become a father. But hear me when I say that bringing up a child, and rearing a family is the ultimate test of man." "The test of man." Cain interrupted scoffing with sarcasm in his voice. "First it was the curse of man, now it is the test of man. Tell me father, how many parts of man are there?" Cain mocked openly with a breath of conceit overly confident that Adam would not be able to answer or respond to the pretentious rhetoric's of his own examination.

Adam refused to be derailed by Cain affronting attempt and considered for a moment to unload the various facets and faces of man. Adam attempted to account the many instances, and scenarios associated with manhood. He lost count midway and was forced to produce a general response. "There are far too many for me to count alone." Adam submitted peacefully. Cain found himself was once again annoyed by his father's ignorant and contemptuous remark. He was overcome with the sudden and unnatural thought of correcting his father's rude and arrogant behavior with a swift blow to his temple. Cain believed the hard thumping would help jog and return the old man back to his senses. However, tempted as he was Cain fought against the swelling urge and unclenched his fisted knuckles disarmed by pity and disappointment at witnessing Adam's descending plight. Cain wanted to speak out and help raise his father from his lowly plight and station but could find any sympathetic words to offer as council. He struggled to convey the appropriate response before heaving a heavy gust of air into his lungs. Dropping his shoulder Cain released an intense filled sigh of exhaustion symbolizing his submission and defeat as he resolved to allow his father to complete his rambunctious ramblings.

"You are of my blood." Adam reminded his son. "You too own a burning desire deep within you. Like a wild beast it hungers for passion and gratification. This beast has yet to be awoken within you, but soon you will witness first-hand the wrath of its might." Cain was a bit irked with the thought of a beast living inside of him taking Adams metaphoric message literally. The troubling thought alone caused Cain to shudder plagued by the course and path of his own imagination. "Learn to conquer the beast from within so that you may be able to overcome the spirit of ills and despair which inhabit this world. Learn to befriend the company of hardship and do not give into discomfort. Expect that trouble will surface to confront you on your path and journey, and place neither blame or fault on pride or shame in times of adversity. And be not coy to retreat when necessary and emerge again when the opportunity calls. Learn to accept defeat and victory with the same weight and breadth of humility."

Cain was clueless as to the direction of his father's narrative but could see that Adam reserved a tone of conviction in his speech. "It is much too late for me." Adam warned gazing directly into the face of his son. The dark rigid corners of his eyes scrunched tightly reflecting the gravity in his message. "I soiled my chastity by allowing myself to be deflowered and seduced. Misguided by my lustful desires and innate proclivity for pursuing worldly pleasure. I allowed myself to be led astray. I let impurity sully my heart and issue my transgressions, unable at the time to deny the sensual touch and caress of flesh. I stumbled upon the unspeakable desires that had never existed in me. When tempted with the opportunity to secure an additional mate to sooth my lustful needs and quell my insatiable hunger. I sought only to rejoice at the favor and generosity being bestowed over me. My feeble appetite for pleasure was served and well fed to the point I found myself losing control becoming powerless in my efforts to turn away or refuse the intoxicating and gentle touch of seduction. By the time I realized what was taking place it was already too late." Adam paused suspensefully. "The beast within me had already taken control of my body."

Adam dropped to the ground and clung tightly to the lifeless body of his mate's body. "I despise myself for being dishonest. It was shameful of me to sully your love with the likes of another." Adam ended his sorrowful confession with a heart wrenching plea for forgiveness. The hysterical conduct of Adam's behavior and pouring outcry was unsavory to say the least. Cain refused to acknowledge his father sobs and was unwilling to offer a hand in aiding Adam back to his feet.

Cain's thoughts seem distracted and stationed elsewhere as he struggled to manage the present crises and events of the day. Adam was overcome with the chilling sensation as though he could somehow feel the frigid glare of Cain's cold dark eyes glaring down at him. The ambience of shameful silence that filled the room was awkward and uncomfortably tense. Adam retracted his arm dismissing any hope for receiving help from his son with getting up the ground. Adam began movingly sluggishly onto his knees than gradually back onto his feet.

Adam found himself standing face to face staring directly into the anguished face of his remaining son. The contours of Cain's bleak face carried the image of a hardened man. He no retained the innocent look of the small boy who Adam happily carried and paraded over his shoulder. Adam struggled to recognize the face of his son beneath the look of pain and anguish etched on his face. He fought to distinguish between the soft gentle eyes of his son and the fierce glaring gaze of his beneficiary. A sudden revelation occurred while searching over the face of his son. Adam took special notice to the erosion of youthful features in Cain's appearance. The armor of youth had been removed exposing the fragile adolescent shell of a bruised and battered man. Cain was emotionally distant and unavailable he had checked out in his passive display of aggression. He was offset by the dissonance of feuding thoughts that plagued his mind feeling somewhat numbed and desensitized by the traumatic turn of events. Cain seem to struggle with reoccurring and intrusive thoughts that filled and caroled his mind and conscious as he was now confronted with the burdening account of his father's admission and guilt.

Cain felt repulsed and somewhat nauseated by the sight of his father. He shifted his gaze away from Adam and stumbled across a strange object lying on the floor near cavern wall. The object drew Cain's attention as he walked over to further investigate. Disconnected in dreamy like daze Cain felt compelled and drawn to the object, ignoring the fading words of Adam voice echoing in the background "I remember myself at your age," Adam recalled. "Strong and vibrant with a host of well to do wishes." Cain's curiosity drew him closer to the sharp object before uncovering the dagger stained with the blood of his beloved mother. He quickly recognized the signature craftsmanship belonging to his father and was instantly consumed with fury and rage. "You see my son..." Adam continued unaware of his sons startling discovery. "...Our natural resemblance serves evident in mirth and substance that you and I are just alike, and in due time you will..."

"Never!" Cain Roared defiantly like a fierce lion confronting an intruder. "I am nothing like you." Cain reproached his father. "You are a fool who has brought death, and dishonor to our home. You are delusional to believe that you loved my mother?" "Of course I loved your mother," Adam answered intuitively in defense of his honor. "It is complicated to explain." Adam pleaded. "You would not understand, you cannot possibly fathom the..." "No," shouted Cain sending his father of his feet with a fierce shove. The forceful push sent Adam tumbling back over the body of his widow. "Not this time." Cain declared refusing to listen any longer to the passive complexities of Adam pleas. "I nearly believed your lies, and almost allowed myself to sympathize in your remorse. But now I see that I was mistaken." Cain's intensity and demeanor was fierce and somewhat troubling with a cold dead glare over his face. He slowly approached Adam drawing closer and more hostile with every step. Adam cowardly retreated crawling backwards on his hands and heels attempting desperately to avoid Cain's advancement and unprovoked confrontation.

"You owe me an explanation!" Cain shouted in a deep fierce voice echoing proudly through the den. The booming command provoked a shuddering sensation to run through his nerves. Adam was gripped with unimaginable fear and terror at the sudden confrontation of his son. Adam seemed baffled and confused as to what prompted the sudden change in Cain attitude. "Why have lashed out at me?" Adam pleaded ignorantly. "Explain as to why your special dagger lays in the same room as my befallen mother?" Without waiting for an explanation Cain pounced on his father overpowering him and seizing him firmly in his grips. Adam struggled to free himself from the fisted hold of his primed son. He was petrified by the intense hostility and deadly show of aggression being demonstrated by his son. Before this moment Adam had never given consideration or thought to the plight of his descent and demise. The image of an untimely death swelled considerably in Adam's mind as he imaged the fatal outcome of his assault at the hands of his son

"My son, do not be angry with me." Adam struggled to speak, "What I intended to say is that with the introduction of Eve, my vision of love became blurred and skewed." "Silence!" Cain snarled unloading blows over his father. "How dare you attempt to diminish your role and responsibility in this whole ordeal." Cain scolded angrily. "You seek to evade accountability for inflicting the fatal wounds which brought an end to mother." Cain accusatory proposition was rather unexpected. "You are truly a monstrous creature the very descendent and child of God." Cain mocked menacingly. "Rather than being a quivering loath of a coward. Why not seize your destiny from God's grips and wield your own path and destiny as you see fit. Why do you allow yourself to be tempted and ensnared by what you describe as the blossom's petals of fleshly caresses. You allowed yourself to be manipulated and easily misguided by your appendage. You willfully steered off course trailing blindly down an unsavory and reckless path. Testify before me and affirm that you are a man and not an incubus of some sorts. Do not be tempted to grovel back to God's feet in search of absolution and forgiveness. We are no longer infants or children requiring the nursing and nurturing of God. We should no longer yearn to be suckled or nestled comfortably by our creators."

Cain seemed oddly displaced with a fiery aura and glow permeating over his body, "For the life of me." He questioned. "I cannot understand why you allow God to use you so!" Cain spoke harshly yelling at Adam as though he was a simple child, "Why do you allow yourself to be subjugated by God's will?" Cain posed the inquiry but received no response or answer from Adam. "Why do you feel the need to bow before his feet?" Cain demanded to know yelling madly at his father exposing his frustration and inner turmoil. Cain soon found his hands firmly gripped around his father neck resisting against the temptation of squeezing breath and life from his father lungs. Cain's fierce and hostile demeanor shook Adam to his core, he no longer found familiarity or safety in the face of present danger. Adam felt ambushed by his son furious assault and pent-up rage.

"You still revere God," Cain taunted. "Despite his unrequited affection for you." Adam could hardly breath struggling to escape smothering grips of Cains hold over him. "Have you ever stopped to consider the reason as to why God created man in his mortal image. It is so he can remove the precious gift of life from us at any moment under his discretion." Adam legs began to falter and buckle slowly. "God fears us." Cain explained. "He fears man because he knows that we have the potential to overtake this world and govern ourselves ruling as we see fit. No longer will we need to seek penance at his feet or plea for his grace or mercy." Cain felt a sense of conviction for his merciless behavior and released his father from the stronghold of his might and grip. Adam could barely stand as he plummeted to the ground and began panting desperately to gather air. Towering over his father Cain extended his arm out to provide Adam support, "Let us work together father." Cain proposed. "So that we may seize this world and transform it into our own paradise and glorious kingdom."

"I am old son.'" Adam pleaded pitifully "I have spent too much of my time at odds with my father nursing anguish. It is sad that it took the tragic loss of my partner and child for me to see the error of my ways and acknowledge my wrongdoings. I have experienced the smite of God far too many times for me to deny his name and very existence. After witnessing firsthand, the precious gift of life be extinguished of its fiery essence. I no longer wish to hold a personal vendetta or host a private war against my God and creator," Adam began to lift himself off the ground, regaining his footing as he spoke candidly, "I have come to terms with my maker, and have come to accept wholeheartedly the purpose of my design. The path of my journey is filled with abundance and hope." Cain did not react contentiously, or attempt lash out and attack Adam. "Do not think it light of me to submit and surrender the ideals that I strived to uphold and protect. The same values which took the lives of your mother, and brother removing their gift of light from this world." Adam, stopped suddenly, "I tussled, and brawled and fought a good fight son." Adam admitted. "And in the end, I won't say that I lost the fight against my creator, but some compromises were made. I have matured since then and gained a better understanding of my relationship with my father. Submission it is not easy however it is necessary to rebuild trust and faith in my creator."

Adam boldly placed his hand over the shoulders of his son, "My hope is that you will learn to forgive your father, as I have learned to forgive my creator. I plead that you do not waste your vibrant years like me moving against the grains and resenting the direction of the clouds above your head." Cain listened to his father words like the reading of a last will and testament. "Come with me." Adam surprisingly suggested, "I can bring you to back to the garden and together we can plead and pray for your merciful forgiveness and salvation..." Cain flared his nostrils and spat at the idea. "I will do no such thing." Cain snapped clearly opposed to the thought. He turned and began walking towards his mother lying stiff on the floor. Cain stood over the body of his departed mother and unfolding his arms he slowly crouched down to pay his final respects. He managed to lift the body of the deceased into his arms in an effortless motion. Cain cradled the lifeless body of his mothers in his arm with ease and little effort. He began to grow rather emotional looking down at his mother nestled tightly in his arms. Cain was saddened by the tender and lifeless face of his slumbering mother who would never again awaken.

"Wait, but where are you going?" Adam stammered. "Do not worry yourself," Cain responded. "We are no longer any concern of yours."

He concluded defiantly with a cold glare that chilled Adam to his core. The cruel tone of Cain's words wounded Adam deeply like a dagger shoved directly into his side. Cain's seasoned remark left a bitter taste in Adams mouth that caused him to spit the curdling taste of blood out onto the floor. "Go on and take your leave." Cain urged his father. "Return to your precious God and fall comfortably back into the trenches of your beloved Eden. But remember, I swear upon my life and the very life of my mother. I will not rest until I enact my revenge upon you all." Cain warned. "Never forget father that it was not I who struck the first blow or committed the initial offense in this unholy war." "Forgiveness is way." Adam conceded. "Forgiveness is the sword which ends all feuds and battles." Adam attempted to reason sensibly with his son but found the fiery freshmen posturing arrogantly into his adolescence phase. The complex transformation brought with it a host of emotional nuances including the newly found desire for autonomy, and independence. "There is no place for forgiveness in my heart when it was not I who hurled the first stone. My vow of vengeance will only end once God your father and creator pleads before my feet for mercy and forgiveness." "Do not be ridiculous," Adam inserted impulsively. "You must be mad if you think that our master and ruler will fall at your feet seeking mercy and forgiveness." "Oh, but he will." "Cain assured maniacally. "For the sake and welfare of his children and their descendants. That is the only way to make amends and secure my pardon."

Adam watched helplessly as his son walked away carrying his mother in his arms. He considered interjecting and demanding that Cain return the body of his beloved partner and mate but was unable to voice his objections. Adam concluded it best not to interfere or impose on the delicate moment. "I may never forgive for your betrayal father." Cain remarked condemning Adam as he drew closer to the exit of the doorway. "Be sure to inform your father, creator, God or what have you, that this feud is not over. I shall have my revenge." Cain ended the discourse of his threats with a bold and daring declaration. Adam sat idle looking at his son's elongated shadow slowly disappearing beneath the peak of light. Adam was taken aback bewildered and astonished by the obscene behavior of an outright madman. "God will never plead at your feet!" Adam brazenly yelled back out addressing no one in particular, "God is our creator, we are not his!" Adam cried out woefully. In looking around and finding himself alone in an empty room, he was fraught with the overwhelming sense of sadness and remorse. It hurt to see his son so entangled and confined by chains of hatred. "He will undoubtedly teach his children the same degree and method of hatred enacting violence and vengeance against God's future descendants. He will propagate and slander the name of my father, defining him as cruel, and unjust establishing God as a cancerous entity that removes life without warrant or reasonable cause."

It became stake painstakingly clear to Adam, that before the dawn of the day he would have ultimately lost both his two sons. One at the hands of death, and the other by way of self-emancipation. Adam contemplated on whether he should wait in the cavern for Cain to return from burying his mother or hasten his retreat from the cavern. He considered the weight of his son's sinister promise of enacting vengeance. Adam wanted nothing more than to mend the growing tension and relationship between a creator and his creation. The traumatic images of Cain's aggressive assault invaded Adam's thoughts causing him to become somewhat unsettled and anxious of Cain's sudden return. Adam was unsure as to the mood or state in which Cain would come to meet him. He began to dread the thought of being isolated and confined in an empty room with his tempered and irritable son. Adam considered the fatal thought that if he provoked his son in any way that it would be his lifeless body lying on the ground next. The dreadful image helped him to decide and make up in his mind about how he would proceed. Adam glanced one last time over the room filled with many warm memories. He looked around at the wall, over the ceiling, and then back down again at the ground.

His eyes spotted the very dagger which had triggered Cain lying on the floor near the wall. Moving closer, Adam uncovered the tool for which he personally carved and help fashion into design. The blade was soaked and stained with the blood of his befallen mate. In his hands Adam was able identify the exact tool in detail and in craftsmanship. "The gift I bestowed onto Eve," Adam thought finding it strange that such a coveted gift could go missing without the slightest bit of commotion.

The image of his mate's being slain with the sharp chiseled dagger was unsettling. The thought alone prompted a shudder and convulsion through his body. Adam fell low in spirit considering that the very tool that forged had been manipulated and misused to help bring a fatal and tragic end to the love of his life. It became apparently clear to him to why God had banished the crafting of weapons in the garden. "I forge this cursed tool." Adam confessed. "And breached the boundaries of my own arrogance by smuggling unsanctioned tool into Eden." The sobering realization of his direct involvement in the slaying of his mate began to dawn over Adam. The very implication helped to fill him with even more regret and guilt if possible. In his mind he could still see vividly the glowing his face mate smiling back at him with charitable beauty. "I was foolish of me to forget why delicate flowers bear the sharpest of thorns. However, you prove to be the flawless exception." Adam concluded his thoughts after sharing some regaling final words to his beloved mate.

In no time Adam was back out on the trail headed back in the direction of Eden. He discarded the sharpened tool swearing off the crafting and forging of tools forever. Adam ran with delegating thoughts on whether to inform Tree, of the dagger he discovered. "And what of Eve." Adam appeared concerned. "The poor creature must be trifled with confusion. I hope she will recover after this intense ordeal." Adam ran back towards Eden moving swiftly as if though he no longer felt secure on the outside of the grand walls. Haunted by an eerie sense of impeding danger Adam hastened his pace and lengthened stride speeding quickly towards the sanctuary and security of Eden where he believed himself to be safe. Adam arrived at the grand walls and entered quickly thru the threshold. He immediately sealed off the door and barred off the gates behind him before releasing a heaving gust of relief.

13

The Conclusion

Adam felt sorrowful for his abrupt departure. Plagued by the thought of his many unfavorable losses. "Both of my sons are gone." Adam grieved mournfully. "Abel through tragic death, while Cains holds me in contempt and spite." He shook his head despairingly recounting the unfortunate set of events that took place throughout the day. "I fear the worst for mankind." Adam cried to himself. "Cain is my flesh and bone, but I worry that his unbridled anger will continue to grow and fester until he is entirely consumed with anger and hatred. If left unchecked his anguish and passion will become the catalyst and driving force drawing him closer to the brink of evil."

"What will become of his offspring's." Adam thought. "And his descendants to follow after? Will they inherit the cancer of hatred, carrying on the legacy of their forefathers?" These thoughts and more surfaced through Adam's mind as he charted the bushy forest of Eden "The fiery anguish of passion burning deep within Cain's heart ignited images foreshadowing his future kin. These masters of architects were skilled at designing and crafting tools and weapons but were unskilled at forging alliances. Creatures with the internal proclivity for destruction and chaos as their preferable path and choice. The descendants of Cain will leave bloodshed, and carnage wherever they are met." Adam considered the senseless genocides and needless holocausts that would surely ensue because of Cains descendant.

Adam hoped that his son would someday seek to repent and accept God's as his lord and savior.

Adam imagined the duration that Cain's long-standing feud with God would rival and carry on for eternity. The cycle of animosity and hatred would eventually spill over onto the children of God. Countless innocent lives will be lost, and many more souls will suffer at the mercy of heartache. "They will eventually come to plunder and pillage like barbarians and savages, killing one another. taking the very life and souls of their kindred brothers." In seeing the divide in the trajectory of his bloodline and lineage Adam became overwhelmed provoked by feelings of grief and anxiety churning deep within him. Adam imagined in his mind a nation and world entirely devoted to the vengeful legacy of their inherent forebears. In his mind he saw the baton of hatred being passed down generational to Cains descendants. Those who reject God and willingly accept other denominations to guide their sacred values and core principle. Adam juxtaposed the outlook and future of his own descendants. He envisioned his decedents as peaceful and pious creatures unequipped and unwilling to spill innocent blood content in their virtue. They were kind and generous beings with high regard for love and life." Troubled by his somber state and ambush of racing thoughts, Adam hurried his pace moving quickly through the jungle in dire council of Tree. Adam intended to meet with Tree for moral support and obtain invaluable guidance and wisdom on the very matter.

Adam could think of no one more equipped than Tree to provide judgment, and sound advice. He refused to tread the same barren and isolated path as that of his vengeful son. Adam feared the uncertainty of his son's promise; unsure whether to believe, or disregard Cain's viable threat. Loneliness coiled over Adam's mind, as he reflected on the untimely death of his mate. A heavy sigh expelled from his nostrils as he recalled some of their fondest moments forever immortalized in his memories. It seemed surreal to Adam that he had lost his entire family in the span of one day. The severe pain and realization left Adam excruciatingly numb and emotionally wounded. Adam meandered through Eden, malingering about the garden oblivious to the world and creatures surrounding him.

One thing was certain that Adam did not want to be alone especially after having loss two sons, and the life of his beloved companion. Adam took solace and comfort in believing that he still retained the friendship and affection of his dear lifelong friend. "I must meet with Tree." Adam regarded. "She will lift my spirits and provide comfort from the aching bitterness which plagues my mind and heart." Adam felt a sense of comfort believing confidently that Tree would be able to sooth his troubled mind. "Tree will surely console me." Adam recited to himself attempting to pacify his racing nerves. "Especially in my moment of desperation and dire time of need."

Adam moved about like a foreigner walking pensively through the familiar forest. He looked queerly at the estranged group of animals as they strolled and pranced casually by him. The animals returned blank looks and gawking stare at Adam however, they did not speak or greet him with kind words in the usual fashion. Unbeknown to Adam the creatures of Eden had all been compromised and made incomparable and unintelligible by the ruthless power of their renowned king. The animals of Eden could no longer communicate or speak clearly to man or any creature outside their own specious. Any creature that attempted to communicate managed only to produce muffled and distorted sounds resembling growls, howls and shrieks and other strange noises. Apparently shortly after removing Tree's voice the king took it upon himself to relegate the voices of all the inhabitants by revoking their ability to communicate speak to man as a necessary measure of precaution. God was prioritizing the need to conduct damage control to maintain the quality and image of his illustrious garden. He was determined to contain and conceal confidentiality over the course of events that transpired on this day. God envisioned that with Eve's compliance and support today's narrative could be changed to exonerate him from having any involvement in Adam's unraveling and undoing. Eve was the only creature that could testify against the king and serve as the voice of truth. However, Eve had already sworn an oath of loyalty pledging her obedience and allegiance to God.

Adam finally arrived finding the garden somewhat quiet, and inactive. There were no loud chattering just strange noises of commotions coming from animals babbling back and forth. The prevalent sounds of shrieks, and howls were heard off in the distance. The snarling sounds of growls, and grunts were vaguely new reception unfamiliar to Adam. He could not gather any content or context from the strange and unfamiliar language. The animals barked and roared at Adam as if attempting to communicate invaluable information of some sorts. Sorely Adam was unable to comprehend or decipher their growls, barks or shrieking cries. Adam was experiencing an unfamiliar form of passive excommunication. The utterances of unfamiliar noises and sounds left Adam confused unsure how to respond to crowd of wailing onlookers. Adam grew perplexed and somewhat annoyed to find that his ability to speak and communicate with the inhabitants and tenants of Eden had been stripped away.

The creatures of Eden had lost their voices all except for Adam and Eve. They received immunity as their voices were preserved to assure effective communication between the two. Eve had pledged her allegiance and eternal service to the king and in exchange she was rewarded the retention of her status as the queen of Eden. This secret pledge to teach her children, and descendants especially her daughters to praise God first and foremost. "Love thy God." served as the mantra for her daughters, while her sons received an equally ominous prescription. "Fear thy God." The regiment of love and fear was intended to keep her children and descendants morally aligned. Adam moved about Eden unaware of the secret treaties and conspiring pledges being formed without his knowledge. He arrived at Tree's site where he found her standing eerie and strangely silent. Her large and hefty stature overshadowed that of the neighboring trees in the vicinity. Adam felt a sense of relief and rejoiced at the sight of his dear friend.

He found himself growing somewhat emotional at the sight of Tree drawing forth tears of joy from his eyes. Adam was like a small child standing before his tender caretaker. Lost feelings of safety and assurance began to surface within Adam's hearth and spirit. He was confident that his loving matriarch would somehow find a way to ease his grief and tension. Adam had grown rather accustomed to relying on Tree to provide council for his troubles. Her sound advice was regarded by Adam as constructive and hopeful. He was optimistic that she would offer a positive spin and outlook to his present dilemma.

Adam soon arrived at Tree's location and rejoiced at finding his dearest and lifelong companion in her allotted station "Tree my dear friend." Adam rejoiced openly. "I am so happy to see you." Adam did not wait for an answer or response before unfurling the troubling events of his day, "Woe is me." Adam cried. "It seems that I have lost all that I hold dear." Adam broke down instantly and began sobbing pitifully before his best friend, "Abel, Cain, and my beloved mate are all gone from me, and I have only myself blame for it. I have forsaken my children and deceived my lover by welcoming the eternal footman into my houses. I managed to humiliate myself and even worse, I tarnished my relationship with my only remaining child. Cain now runs wild with an anguish and vengeance coiled over in his heart." Adam stewed in self-pity seeming unfazed by the reception of silence he received. He accepted Tree's silent review as a mutable gesture and affirmation taking little notice to the apparent change in Tree's silent and poised demeanor.

"The fault is all mine," Adam continued his confession, "I never should have attempted to live as I had, preoccupied with duality and consumed by my own selfish interests. I have forsaken my family and severed the bonds of trust and love we once shared." Adam looked up at Tree, drawn inaudibly by the sheer volume of her and silence. Tree did not speak but stood staring down at Adam with a blank look and expression over her face. Tree could not comfort her beloved friend although she wanted desperately to offer aid to him. She wished for nothing more than to console her dearest Adam letting him know that he was not the blame, or anyway at fault for the unfortunate events that had occurred and taken place. "I am baffled by the path that led to my corruption." Adam cried out. "I did not want to become like my father, but now it seems that I am more like my creator than anything else." Tears began to form in his eyes and very soon flooded his face. "My youngest son has passed, and so has my beloved mate and partner. Cain my only surviving heir despises me such that he will not speak to me." "Please Tree." Adam begged growing inpatient and somewhat annoyed by her silent reaction and display. "Offer me some kind words to take refuge. Please do not ignore or turn your back to me like this cold uncaring world. You are the only one that I have left who truly understands and cares for me."

Adam wallowed and pleaded tirelessly however Tree could not break the silent curse and hold over her. In misinterpreting the situation Adam began to grow rather frustrated and annoyed with his friend. "Please speak to me Tree." Adam urged on. "It appears as if the entire garden shuns me today. Please Tree do not shun me as well." He fell onto his knees and began to weep sorrowfully "It is I your precious Adam can you not recall." Adam stretched out his arms to offer a hug and warm embrace coddling over Tree's large robust body. His secured his arms firmly around at the waist of her large trunk. Tree was filled with sorrow emotionally moved by the sentimental gesture which drew tears from her eyes. The moist dew that seeped from her eyes traveled the wrinkles of her bark skin flowing down to her roots. Adam could feel the warm dew of dampened moisture streaming down his face.

"I am sorry Tree." Adam cried out. "If I have wronged you in anyway. "Please forgive me." Adam sobbed repeatedly for Tree to respond to his pouring outcry. Adam was in dire need of consoling and sought the council and company of his dearest friend for support. They were left with no remaining options between them except to revel in the overwhelming feeling of defeat and disappointment. Adam felt heartbroken and emotionally torn uncertain of what to do next. The mild irritation of salty tears began to obscure and blur his vision. Adam placed his head over his arms in an avid attempt to hide his face from the prying eyes of onlookers. Adam was distraught to point that he did not notice or draw attention to Eve making a stealthy appearance. She stood quietly to the side peering down over him. "Do not cry Adam." Assured the familiar voice. "I have not forsaken you." Adam quickly recognized the soft voice and was immediately overcome with excitement. "Eve!" Adam rejoiced happily delighted to hear the voice and sound of another.

The intense proceedings of the day caused Adam to cast Eve into the background of his mind. His thoughts were very much consumed by the present state of grief and disappointment. In all his misery and trouble, he had vaguely forgotten to search and call out to her. However, at seeing Eve standing before him Adam took considerable notice to the glow of her beauty beneath the radiant sun. Eve moved in closer to Adam and slowly extended her arms to him. He seized and gripped her hands in an accepting and supportive gesture back to his feet. "I have heard your weeping cries." Eve answered. "I am deeply afflicted by your sorrows. I beg that you do not blame yourself for the unfortunate turn of events that have occurred." Gazing deep into Adam's face Eve saw herself reflected through the mirror of moisture that swelled beneath his eyes. Eve could vividly see the pain, anguish, guilt and shame which Adam tried desperately to hide. The burden of emotional baggage he shouldered and carried appeared overwhelming and daunting. Adam was depleted and felt entirely spent from the exhausting events of the day. Eve recognized with ease the painful look of grief and turmoil entrenched on Adams face. The burden of shame and guilt resonated empathetically between the two creatures with each carrying their burden of emotional baggage for the ordeal. Eve mirrored the sum of Adams sorrow and heartache with both creatures feeling somewhat tormented and isolated inside.

Adam stood before Eve like a child sulking woefully. The image alone evoked a sense of pity and sympathy from Eve. Witnessing Adam in such a lowly state and plight brought neither joy nor fulfillment to Eve. At seeing Adam in a visible state of pain and anguish Eve considered for a moment whether to betray her interest and reveal the truth to him. Eve decided that it was best not disclose the secret pact and promise made between her and the king. Eve vowed before God never to not disclose the truth to Adam. However, history would come to record the breach of confidentiality that would result in both Eve and Adam being exiled and banished from Eden. The sacred contract and royal seal would one day be torn in bad faith ultimately tarnishing God's relationship with mankind. Adam and Eve's eventful fall from grace would occur centuries later. However, in the present moment Eve was choosing to uphold and honor the sacred vow and agreement contracted between herself and her creator.

"I still love you Adam," She confessed openly, "I have never stop loving you." Eve softly wiped away the remaining tears from Adam's face. "You are kind, and you are charitable," Eve declared. Her kind words of affirmation helped to restore Adam's sense of pride and good nature. "You are virtuous and wise, strong, and proud. You have vast knowledge and wisdom with a keen observation of discernment. You are a good father, and a wonderful provider please do not allow this incident to convince you otherwise." Eve's soothing words helped to ease the burden of shame and guilt that Adam carried inside him. The gesture of kindness served as a useful coping tool to lighten the load of grief and sorrow weighing over his heart. Adam's tragic defeat and personal failings produced with him a victim mindset that aligned perfectly with the outcome of his lowly descent. Eve unlike Adam was filled with hope and optimism about the future ahead of them. She surrendered her sorrow and will over to her master and king in exchange for better days to come. Adam soon found himself gazing helplessly into Eve's eyes. He listened without objection to the list his positive qualities observed since their initial interaction. "Your resilience and determination by way of overcoming obstacles in order thrive and not just survive harsh climates and conditions is truly unparalleled." Eve's high praise and regard was met with a disarming smile. "Despite facing hardships and being constantly confronted with misfortune and adversity you always manage to find a way and means to overcome. That is what truly defines and sets you apart from any other being." Eve broke her gaze no longer able bear the irritation of guilt gnawing at her conscious, "I am sorry Adam for everything that has happened." She rested her head gently against his broad chest, "I can see that you are hurting right now, allow me to sooth your wounds and ease your pain."

Adam did not respond but stood stoically entranced by the depth and range of his own thoughts. He was void to the warm invitation and generous proposition offered by Eve. Adam's deflated demeanor only helped to demonstrate his indifference in the matter. His desire for Eve had slowly subsided behind a veil of nagging thoughts and fleeting insecurities. Adam found himself at an impasse. His hesitation was seen as rejection which drew further embarrassment to the awkwardness of the moment. Eve reacted emotionally to Adam's display and lagging of interest. Adam appeared distracted navigating between the realms of his imagination and consciousness. He drew confusion over the status of his present position. Adam could not help looking at Eve without seeing the face and image of his former partner. He was now burdened with remorse for his sinful conduct and infidelity. Adam viewed his actions through the lenses of prudence and integrity. He condemned the frequency of moonlit trysts and voyages he willingly embarked on. Adam began to feel somewhat irritated by his inability to tame and control his lustful desires.

Suddenly without warning Adam sprang wildly clutching onto Eve's face. Their lips clenched together in a passionate interlocking. The tender kiss sent a jolt of electricity through Eves body traveling down her back and spine. The salty taste of Adam lips did not discourage Eve from welcoming the pleasant embrace of his touch. She wrapped her arms around Adam's body holding him firmly with her face nestled comfortably between his shoulders. Eve began to hum a familiar tune that was taught to her by Tree. The childhood melody was regarded as Adam's favorite song that helped to sooth and quell his restless nerves. In a strange turn of events, it appeared that Eve would hold the final note and outcome. Adam reserved mixed feelings towards Eve recalling his harsh and unjust mistreatment towards her. He feared that the roller coaster of emotional betrayal and turmoil she endured on his behalf had not been entirely forgiven. Adam reflected on the times when he held little interest in Eve often feeling repulsed by the presence of her company. He remembered ignoring Eve often many times intentionally to discourage their engagement and inter-action.

However, in the present moment Adam was grateful that he was not alone, "I am happy that you are here," Adam thanked Eve, "I never imagined that of all God's creatures that it would be you to rescue me from the lowly abyss of sadness." He was observing the delicacy of life through its natural cycle and order. Adam began to accept his obliga-tion and assigned role, taking valuable lessons from the surrounding nature. Just as a beautiful paradise and garden can be formed from a single small seed, so was Adam moved to attempt once again to cul-tivate and grow his family by taking Eve as his queen. "Even after my disregard and neglect." Adam spoke regretfully. "You manage to exer-cise kindness and compassion over me." He was moved to tears. "I will always love you," Eve reassured Adam. Their bodies bundled closely together into perfect symmetric union. "This time I hope you do not forget it." Eve teased Adam playfully in good spirit and humor. The warm flowery scent of her hair brought with it a delightfully sooth-ing fragrance and aroma that seem to arouse Adams senses. His de-sire for Eve seemed more potent than ever before. "I do not want to be alone." Adam confessed openly to Eve. "To live my days as a rogue wanderer..." "You do not have to" Eve quickly reassured him, "Let us evade loneliness and isolation and live together in this very paradise or any setting you deem fit. I am prepared to follow you to the ends of the world my beloved partner and mate." The title seemed strange and oddly endearing to hear on the receiving end. "Yes." Adam rejoiced happily. "We will stay here in the paradise created and designed to house us."

Their bodies gathered like silhouettes before the golden sun. Adam grabbed Eve by the waistline and kissed her passionately. He pulled away his face only to steal another glimpse into her soft eyes. Adam felt remarkably blessed and fortunate to have Eve at his side. Adam and Eve held onto one another for what seemed like an eternity with neither wanting to be the first to detach or sever the tender moment and bond.

-End

Prince Otchere is a contemporary African author with deep spiritual and religious ties to the Christian apologetic faith. His eclectic style of writing and storytelling is uniquely tailored to Christ conscious readers, and those seeking spiritual wisdom, understanding. Prince writes religiously with the intention of liberating audiences and followers from post-modern ideology that inhibit spiritual growth and development. Raised predominantly in the Christian faith, Prince draws his inspiration from the Genesis story and now looks to add meaning and depth to the classic biblical story and historical tale. Prince has professional experience in the field of behavioral mental health with a master's level education in the field of Social Work. Prince is a visionary writer whose profound works offers conventional gems of wisdom as well as guidance to readers through his unique style of writing and storytelling. Prince draws his insight from a combination of spaces including social, personal, professional and spiritual life. An author and a collector of human experiences, Prince possesses the keen skills of observation and empathy which he utilizes in his interpretation and retelling of famous historical events and stories. Prince is an existentialist writer who work explore parallels between human experience and religious ideology which governs human behavior. Prince writes candidly to his audience in a genuine and authentic narrative that helps to highlight the integrity and truth of his message. Prince has an empathetic unique writing style that allows him to channel his imagination and senses beyond the boundaries of space and time.